Wind over
 and Other D

*Also from
Bruce Holland Rogers:*

Flaming Arrows
Bedtime Stories to Darken Your Dreams (editor)

Wind over Heaven
and Other Dark Tales

Bruce Holland Rogers

WILDSIDE PRESS
Berkeley Heights, New Jersey 2000

Wind over Heaven and Other Stories © 2000 Bruce Holland Rogers; all rights reserved.

Rights inquiries should go to the author's agent, Shawna McCarthy of the McCarthy Literary Agency.

Various items in this book appeared elsewhere, over the last so many years; their original copyright dates and publication information follow:

"An Eye for Acquisitions" first appeared in Witch Fantastic, edited by Mike Resnick & Martin H. Greenberg, DAW Books, 1995. Copyright © 1995 by Bruce Holland Rogers.

"Cloud Stalking Mice" first appeared in Cat Crimes Through Time, edited by Ed Gorman, Martin H. Greenberg and Larry Segriff, Carroll & Graf, 1999. Copyright © 1999 by Bruce Holland Rogers.

"Gravity" first appeared in Magic Realism, Spring 1994. Copyright © 1994 by Bruce Holland Rogers.

"Bright Seeds in a Whirlwind" first appeared in The Fortune Teller, edited by Lawrence Schimel & Martin H. Greenberg, DAW Books, 1995. Copyright © 1995 by Bruce Holland Rogers.

"Vox Domini" first appeared in Full Spectrum 4, edited by Lou Aronica, Amy Stout & Betsy Mitchell, Bantam Spectra, 1993. Copyright © 1993 by Bruce Holland Rogers.

"The Dead Boy at Your Window" first appeared in The North American Review, November/December 1998. Copyright © 1998 by Bruce Holland Rogers.

"These Shoes Strangers Have Died Of" first appeared in Enchanted Forests, edited by Katherine Kerr & Martin H. Greenberg, DAW Books, 1995. Copyright © 1995 by Bruce Holland Rogers.

"On Top" first appeared in Imagination Fully Dilated 2, edited by Elizabeth Engstrom, IFD Publishing, 2000. Copyright © 2000 by Bruce Holland Rogers.

"The Apple Golem" first appeared in Xanadu 2, edited by Jane Yolen, Tor, 1995. Copyright © 1995 by Bruce Holland Rogers.

"Wind Over Heaven" first appeared in Diagnosis: Terminal, edited by F. Paul Wilson, Forge, 1996. Copyright © 1996 by Bruce Holland Rogers.

Wind over Heaven and Other Dark Tales
ISBN: 1-58715-118-9
An original publication of
Wildside Press
P.O. Box 45
Gillette, NJ 07933-0045
www.wildsidepress.com

FIRST EDITION

This book is dedicated to Sitka in the hope that she will now leave me the hell alone while I am writing.

Table of Contents

Introduction: Listen Carefully 9
by Alan Rodgers

The Dead Boy at Your Window 11
Vox Domini 15
An Eye for Acquisitions 45
Cloud Stalking Mice 57
Gravity 73
On Top 77
The Apple Golem 97
Wind over Heaven 103
Bright Seeds in a Whirlwind 117
These Shoes Strangers Have Died Of 137

Introduction: Listen Carefully
by Alan Rodgers

You know, I'm not sure how to introduce you to the work of Bruce Holland Rogers.

In the one hand, he's become a moderately well-known writer; routinely he's a finalist for awards like the Nebula, the Stoker, the Edgar Allen Poe Award; he's even won a few here and there. A good many folks have noticed his work and recommended it to one another; it's not as though no one knows who he is.

And still.

I've read a lot of the pap that gets considered — and sometimes even wins! — those awards. Anyone who's been around a bit knows that the awards are almost as apt to speak to a writer's gift for glad-handing as they are to speak to his ability to *write*.

What I need to tell you is that if you haven't read Bruce Holland Rogers, no matter what you're thinking of him, you're wrong.

When I was a baby editor at *Twilight Zone* in the eighties, I saw something that disturbed me. I read everything that went through there, several times in the course of reading and rereading the proofs; and by the time an issue would come out, I'd have a deep, intimate, and personal sense of exactly the quality of every story we'd publish.

I knew where the bodies were buried. I couldn't help knowing.

We published a lot of wonderful stories. We also published things I didn't think much of when I first read them, and came to despise as I read them over and over and over.

And then when the issue came out, I'd see what people responded to — what got the award attention, who got noticed.

What people talked about.

And you know something? The stories that get the awards are not the good ones. Awards go mostly to established writers with a gift for glad-handing; the really, really good stories are almost always

Wind over Heaven

written by some desperate young writer trying to get started — and maybe, maybe, the best of those begin to get folks noticed, if they're persistent, and if they keep reaching for the carousel's brass ring.

This is the thing I need to tell you about Bruce: he's better than the award attention that he gets. The plain fact is that Bruce is a writer so extraordinarily good that he is not at all of a cloth with the people you might consider his peers.

Bruce is *that* good.

He is a body who has things to tell us that we can only dread to know; a writer who has looked into the heart of the world and whispers things we have to know, but fear.

Listen to him carefully. The man's got something to say, and you need to hear it all.

The Dead Boy at Your Window

In a distant country where the towns had improbable names, a woman looked upon the unmoving form of her newborn baby and refused to see what the midwife saw. This was her son. She had brought him forth in agony, and now he must suck. She pressed his lips to her breast.

"But he is dead!" said the midwife.

"No," his mother lied. "I felt him suck just now." Her lie was as milk to the baby, who really was dead but who now opened his dead eyes and began to kick his dead legs. "There, do you see?" And she made the midwife call the father in to know his son.

The dead boy never did suck at his mother's breast. He sipped no water, never took food of any kind, so of course he never grew. But his father, who was handy with all things mechanical, built a rack for stretching him so that, year by year, he could be as tall as the other children.

When he had seen six winters, his parents sent him to school. Though he was as tall as the other students, the dead boy was strange to look upon. His bald head was almost the right size, but the rest of him was thin as a piece of leather and dry as a stick. He tried to make up for his ugliness with diligence, and every night he was up late practicing his letters and numbers.

His voice was like the rasping of dry leaves. Because it was so hard to hear him, the teacher made all the other students hold their breaths when he gave an answer. She called on him often, and he was always right.

Naturally, the other children despised him. The bullies sometimes waited for him after school, but beating him, even with sticks, did him no harm. He wouldn't even cry out.

One windy day, the bullies stole a ball of twine from their teacher's desk, and after school, they held the dead boy on the ground with his arms out so that he took the shape of a cross. They ran a stick in through his left shirt sleeve and out through the right. They stretched his shirt tails down to his ankles, tied everything in place, fastened the ball of twine to a buttonhole, and launched him. To their delight, the dead boy made an excellent kite. It only added to their pleasure to see that owing to the weight of his head, he flew upside down.

When they were bored with watching the dead boy fly, they let go of the string. The dead boy did not drift back to earth, as any ordinary kite would do. He glided. He could steer a little, though he was mostly at the mercy of the winds. And he could not come down. Indeed, the wind blew him higher and higher.

The sun set, and still the dead boy rode the wind. The moon rose and by its glow he saw the fields and forests drifting by. He saw mountain ranges pass beneath him, and oceans and continents. At last the winds gentled, then ceased, and he glided down to the ground in a strange country. The ground was bare. The moon and stars had vanished from the sky. The air seemed gray and shrouded. The dead boy leaned to one side and shook himself until the stick fell from his shirt. He wound up the twine that had trailed behind him and waited for the sun to rise. Hour after long hour, there was only the same grayness. So he began to wander.

He encountered a man who looked much like himself, a bald head atop leathery limbs. "Where am I?" the dead boy asked.

The man looked at the grayness all around. "Where?" the man said. His voice, like the dead boy's, sounded like the whisper of dead leaves stirring.

A woman emerged from the grayness. Her head was bald, too, and her body dried out. "This!" she rasped, touching the dead boy's shirt. "I remember this!" She tugged on the dead boy's sleeve. "I had a thing like this!"

"Clothes?" said the dead boy.

"Clothes!" the woman cried. "That's what it is called!"

More shriveled people came out of the grayness. They crowded close to see the strange dead boy who wore clothes. Now the dead boy knew where he was. "This is the land of the dead."

"Why do you have clothes?" asked the dead woman. "We came here with nothing! Why do you have clothes?"

"I have always been dead," said the dead boy, "but I spent six years among the living."

"Six years!" said one of the dead. "And you have only just now come to us?"

"Did you know my wife?" asked a dead man. "Is she still among the living?"

Bruce Holland Rogers

"Give me news of my son!"

"What about my sister?"

The dead people crowded closer.

The dead boy said, "What is your sister's name?" But the dead could not remember the names of their loved ones. They did not even remember their own names. Likewise, the names of the places where they had lived, the numbers given to their years, the manners or fashions of their times, all of these they had forgotten.

"Well," said the dead boy, "in the town where I was born, there was a widow. Maybe she was your wife. I knew a boy whose mother had died, and an old woman who might have been your sister."

"Are you going back?"

"Of course not," said another dead person. "No one ever goes back."

"I think I might," the dead boy said. He explained about his flying. "When next the wind blows. . . ."

"The wind never blows here," said a man so newly dead that he remembered wind.

"Then you could run with my string."

"Would that work?"

"Take a message to my husband!" said a dead woman.

"Tell my wife that I miss her!" said a dead man.

"Let my sister know I haven't forgotten her!"

"Say to my lover that I love him still!"

They gave him their messages, not knowing whether or not their loved ones were themselves long dead. Indeed, dead lovers might well be standing next to one another in the land of the dead, giving messages for each other to the dead boy. Still, he memorized them all. Then the dead put the stick back inside his shirt sleeves, tied everything in place, and unwound his string. Running as fast as their leathery legs could manage, they pulled the dead boy back into the sky, let go of the string, and watched with their dead eyes as he glided away.

He glided a long time over the gray stillness of death until at last a puff of wind blew him higher, until a breath of wind took him higher still, until a gust of wind carried him up above the grayness to where he could see the moon and the stars. Below he saw moonlight reflected in the ocean. In the distance rose mountain peaks. The dead boy came to earth in a little village. He knew no one here, but he went to the first house he came to and rapped on the bedroom shutters. To the woman who answered, he said, "A message from the land of the dead," and gave her one of the messages. The woman wept, and gave him a message in return.

Wind over Heaven

House by house, he delivered the messages. House by house, he collected messages for the dead. In the morning, he found some boys to fly him, to give him back to the wind's mercy so he could carry these new messages back to the land of the dead.

So it has been ever since. On any night, head full of messages, he may rap upon any window to remind someone — to remind you, perhaps — of love that outlives memory, of love that needs no names.

Vox Domini

In a canyon of blue sandstone, a man is digging a hole. It's a deep hole, long and narrow. It could hardly be anything other than a grave.

There's a stream flowing nearby. Overhead, the sky is tinted orange with dust, with the color of the setting sun. The wind is blowing hard up there. In this region of the planet, the wind always blows hard at sunset. But down here in the canyon, at the base of these high blue walls, the air hardly stirs.

There is no sound but the soft snick *of the shovel cutting through the sand.*

‡

Mohr half opened his eyes when he felt Boursai wiping his mouth again. The cloth was cold and rough, but Boursai was gentle with it.

"That's better," Boursai said. "Isn't that better?"

Mohr tried to turn his back on Boursai, but he was still too drugged, too weak. All he could manage was to turn his head and face the other way.

The light coming through the open doorway was brilliant. The blue cliffs and canyons looked washed out and unreal in the distance. There by the door were the remains of the yellow hexes, tiny cracked shells like dead insects. And between the doorway and the cot where Mohr was lying there was the still-damp spot where Boursai had tried to scrape the floor clean.

"Do you want some water to drink?" said Boursai. "It will wash away the bitterness from your mouth."

But not from my soul, Mohr thought. And then he thought to himself, *Shut up. Stop thinking.*

Mohr heard water trickling from one of the jugs, and then Boursai was in front of him again with a cup in his black hands.

"Take it. Drink."

Mohr closed his eyes and gestured toward the door.

"Gabriel, drink it."

Mohr tried to lift his arms to tap a message into his wrist communicator, but he couldn't manage it. He flicked his wrist impatiently toward the door again.

"I'll go soon enough, Gabriel," said Boursai. "But I must attend to some things first. You've been letting things go around here." He held out the cup. "You need to take better care of yourself and your trees. You've been neglecting your trees, Gabriel."

Mohr tried again to bring his right hand to the keyboard on his wrist. This time he managed to type in a message by feel. Boursai leaned forward to read it. It said: "FUCK TREES."

"You don't mean that. They'll die. Your trees need you, Gabriel."

Mohr keyed in another message. It said, "GO AWAY. DONT CALL ME GABRIEL. GO."

"It's a good name," Boursai said. "It was the angel Gabriel who brought God's words to the prophet, and . . ."

Mohr tried to tune him out. He didn't want to hear more talk of God and the prophet, and he didn't want to hear his name again. Gabriel. His adopted name, the name the Catholics had given him. The name for the fool who had wasted years and years listening for the voice of God. Gabriel. The name Tireen had liked so much. Mohr felt his body stiffen, his heart accelerate. Tireen. Damn Boursai for that, for making him think of Tireen.

Summoning all his strength, Mohr lifted his arm to knock the cup from Boursai's hand.

He keyed the communicator to display, "GO AWAY" and to keep scrolling those words across its screen. Then he closed his eyes and slept.

‡

When Mohr woke, Boursai was not in the room, but Mohr could hear him moving outside in the compound. The wind had come up, blowing so hard that it had to be mid-afternoon.

Boursai moved for a moment to where Mohr could see him framed by the doorway. The man stood swaying in the wind like some tall, black sapling. On his back he carried a water tank, and in one hand he held the dripping nozzle.

Mohr sat up slowly, making the cot creak. His head throbbed, and his body felt like it was made of rags. He looked around the room. Everything had been ordered, tidied up. Even the litter of empty hexes by the door had disappeared. Mohr reached into the breast pocket of his fatigues.

There was nothing there.

Bruce Holland Rogers

He patted the pocket to make sure, then pushed himself up from the cot and shuffled to his foot locker. It was unlocked. He *never* left it unlocked. He touched his neck, feeling for the string that held his key. It was gone.

Hands shaking, he threw the locker open. The bag had been right on top. But not any more.

The empty water tank scraped on the ground outside. Boursai came in, ducking through the doorway.

Mohr punched keys on his wrist. Then he shook the word at Boursai. "WHERE?"

Boursai stepped close. Too close. Mohr turned his face away and keyed in, "GET AWAY!" His hands were shaking. "WHERES STASH?"

Boursai, arms extended as if to catch him, said, "Careful! You shouldn't be on your feet so soon."

Mohr started to key something in, then stopped. This was taking too long, punching one key at a time. He half walked, half stumbled past Boursai to the com-link sitting beside his sink. He switched it on and typed in: "If I fall, it's my own business! If I want to god damn take a fistful of hex and god damn die, that's my own business! Where the hell is my stash?"

Boursai stood just close enough to read the screen. "I took them away," he said. "I put them somewhere."

Mohr glared at Boursai as he typed in: "I suppose you think you're doing me a favor! I'm an addict. Hex is something I need!" He held down the word repeat key so that the screen filled with, "need! need! need! need!"

"I'll give them to you," Boursai said quietly. "I'll give you one a day."

Mohr closed his eyes. His hands felt rubbery. "Thief!" he typed. "What did the prophet say about thieves?"

"I'm sure you know the words of the prophet as well as I do," said Boursai.

"Did once. Trying to forget such crap. Give me my hexes."

Boursai's answer was a soft, "No."

Mohr brought his trembling hands to his face, then raised them in a frustrated, angry gesture. Why are you doing this to me?

"All men are brothers," said Boursai.

Mohr spun back to the keyboard. "Bullshit! All men are brothers, the beloved children of God? Hah! God's gone, Boursai! God's in hiding!"

"It's a wondrous universe, Gabriel. Even if God is remote." Boursai thought for a moment and said, "Isn't this planet proof to you of God's benevolence?"

Mohr shook his head. He had heard this argument before. Not from Boursai, but from other recruits to the Planters Corps. Onazuka's World did seem like a Godsend to some. It was a world with an earth-like atmosphere but with almost no native life forms, the perfect place to colonize. But how had this wonderful situation come into being? Onazuka's World had evolved over billions of years, just like the earth. Artifacts and bones only a few hundred years old showed that there had been a rich and varied biosphere here, the product of an evolutionary process that was just beginning to produce tool makers. In fact, it seemed there were several tool-making species. And then, just centuries before the first humans set foot on this world, a massive meteor collided with the planet, cloaking it in dust. The planet froze. When the dust settled out and the surface warmed again, few native species came back. It was like the world had been made and wiped clean for humanity to colonize with earth life.

"Benevolence?" Mohr tapped in. "A God who murders a world for our convenience is benevolent?"

"If you are as cynical as you seem," Boursai said, "then why did you enlist in the Planters Corps?"

Because, Mohr thought, I wanted to get out of the Live Free Cluster, out of all of the clusters, if I could find a way. I wanted to make planet fall. Any planet fall. And because the recruiter showed me the biggest bag of yellow hex that I had ever seen and said the magic words: Signing bonus. But what he typed was, "None of your damn business. Give me my hex and get out!"

"You're a good planter," Boursai said. "Until recently, you've always been very careful with your trees. Whenever I came to see you, you would be at work."

That's because they'll send me back to Onazuka City if I don't do a good job, Mohr thought. Or back to the clusters. But he had no stomach for explaining things to Boursai. "Come on!" he typed. "Give me my hex and get out! Out! I want to be left alone!"

Mohr turned to look at the other man. He could read the thought in Boursai's eyes: If I'd left you alone today, you'd be dead. But Boursai didn't say this. He didn't have a chance, because at that moment, his wristwatch began to sing in Arabic. His electronic muezzin was calling him to prayer. He excused himself and went outside, consulting the display on his wrist to see what sector of the sky he should face for his obeisance to earth, to Mecca.

Mohr staggered to the door to shut it behind the man, but instead he leaned in the doorway to look out at the blue cliffs, to think of

Bruce Holland Rogers

the canyons where he sometimes planted his trees. The coolness of those streams. The solitude.

While Boursai prayed, Mohr thought of Tireen again, and something stabbed at his heart.

Long ago, when Mohr had gone to the Holy Cluster of the Catholic Church, an old woman named Sister Sarah Theresa had been assigned to instruct him. She was little more than a body suit stretched over bones, and her hair was too white and too thin to hide her skull. She was, secretly, a heretic.

The stabbing in his heart made Mohr think of her now. "It's like a worm in your heart, Gabriel," she had told him. They were floating in the zero-g cathedral — so many religions put their holy places in the hubs of their clusters, as if weightlessness put them closer to God. Mohr and Sister Sarah Theresa were in the apse, looking at the statue of the Son of God and Man. Stars wheeled slowly by in the windows behind the Saviour's head.

"The catechism teaches that there is no guilt," the old woman said, looking around to see that she was not overheard. They were, in fact, alone in the cathedral. "They say now that there is only Affective Spiritual Dissonance." She chuckled. "They water God down until there is nothing left but psychology." Then, more seriously, she pointed a bony finger: "There *is* guilt, Gabriel. It's like a worm eating away at your heart from the inside. God can take away that worm, but you have to confess. You have to speak aloud what sin you have committed, in the hearing of another human being."

"Why must it be spoken?" Mohr had asked her.

"Because that's the only way to release what's in your heart. That's the only way God will hear you. Speak aloud what you have done — you can't just think it or write it. It's still in your heart, then. You have to confess. The heart and the tongue are connected. When you confess, you poison that worm in your heart with truth."

Boursai was finishing his prayer, and Mohr felt the stab in his heart once more. He remembered the way that Tireen had clawed at his hand on the airlock button, then on the override switch. He remembered the look in her eyes. The disbelief. He remembered what the vacuum did to her face. Guilt is a worm. Guilt is a worm. Confess, Gabriel Mohr!

But he would have to use words for that, wouldn't he? Spoken words. That's what it would take to confess.

He reached into his pocket out of reflex. If only he could shut off this chatter in his head, these memories! His knees had weakened, and as he slid toward the ground, he felt Boursai's grip seize him.

Wind over Heaven

Touching him. Boursai was touching him.

Mohr pulled away, felt the bile rising in his throat. But his stomach was empty. He only gagged. He thought, half amused, *It's nothing personal, Boursai, you thieving bastard. It's just that I can't stand human beings.* He smiled weakly.

"Come back inside," Boursai said. "Lie down." He offered his hand to help Mohr up. Mohr looked at the hand. No, his reaction to Boursai was more than his ordinary revulsion. There was something about Boursai that made him cringe.

Mohr got to his feet without help. He went back to the com-link. "You're the problem, Boursai. When you don't come around, I need one hex a day, maybe two. But you visit and I take four, I take five or six." He pounded the counter next to the keyboard. "Leave me alone! Give me my hex and go!"

"I will go," Boursai answered, "but I cannot return your drugs to you."

Mohr picked up an empty water jug and hurled it. It went wide of Boursai's head.

"I am sorry for this," Boursai said.

Mohr waved angrily, as if to say, Just get the hell out!

The door closed. Mohr waited a few minutes, then went outside. The wind gusted and Mohr flinched. He didn't like wind. In the clusters, he had never felt more breeze than the gentle exhalations of the ventilation shafts.

Boursai was already a small figure striding near the horizon.

Mohr went back inside and checked under the convex bottom of one water jug, and then reached into the space between the counter and the wall, and then checked the hole he had hollowed out from the dirt floor and covered with a stone. They were all there, his emergency stashes. Boursai hadn't found any of them, probably hadn't thought to look.

First Mohr refilled his breast pocket, then put a hex between his teeth and cracked it. He inhaled through his mouth, felt the warmth travel down his throat, into his lungs and body. Then he spit the empty yellow shell onto the floor.

He looked at the bag and felt his pocket. This supply wouldn't last long. He'd have to convince Boursai to return the rest. What was it with that man, anyway? Why did he insist on coming around here? He had his own compound to attend to, his own trees to get into the ground. Maybe Boursai was lonely. It was just the two of them for a hundred miles in any direction. So what? It wasn't Mohr's fault if Boursai couldn't take a little solitude.

Mohr closed his eyes, and Tireen's face floated up from his

memory. Damn Boursai. Damn him! Mohr cracked another hex.

‡

The sun wasn't quite setting when Mohr turned on his com-link and opened a channel to Boursai. Mohr hardly ever turned his unit on, but now he had a reason. He couldn't stop thinking of that bag of hex.

"Boursai," he transmitted, "bring back my property."

The red contact light came on as Boursai turned on his machine miles away and received the message. And his reply came an instant later: "You took an overdose."

"That's my damn business," Mohr wrote, then wiped it out and replaced it with, "I need the stuff."

"You think you need it."

"I *need* it, Boursai. Return it!"

"Why? Why are you convinced you need to poison yourself?"

Mohr stared at the screen for a moment. If Boursai knew even half of Mohr's story, the ways people had changed him, the things they had done to him, the things *he* had done . . .

"It may make you feel good for a little while," Boursai's message continued, "but it could kill you. It almost did."

That was the idea, Mohr thought. Poison wasn't such a bad idea. If Boursai only knew . . .

"You've got to adjust to this world, Gabriel."

Adjust! That's what he had done more than anyone else he knew, adjusting to one cluster after another. The only place he hadn't really tried to fit in was Holdham, his home cluster, and the only reason he couldn't fit in there was because he happened to be curious about the wrong things! "Where do you get those ideas, boy?" his instructors asked him. And when he told them, they'd say something like, "Those entries ought to be wiped from the encyclopedia. That's ancient history. Useless stuff."

No one else on Holdham was interested in religion. Holdham was a poor cluster, one that barely clung to existence by making its organic cycle as efficient as could be. "There's no room for nonsense in Holdham," his teachers said. "If you can't count it, it isn't real. Spend your time studying Life Support. That's your religion."

But there were questions Mohr wanted answers for, questions that were only half-formed in his mind. Since no one on Holdham even thought the questions were worth asking, he applied to emigrate.

It wasn't easy to get out. The Holdham Cluster saw Mohr as an investment. Not only was his body a storehouse of valuable organics, he was the product of long schooling as a Life Support engineer. But he insisted, and they had to let him go. The laws of the Great Swarm applied to every cluster. Every person had the right to choose another cluster in the Swarm.

The Catholics were the first to take Mohr in. They paid the cost of ferrying him from the Holdham Cluster to their own. Most of the religious clusters would pay this expense, happy to have a convert.

Boursai's words were still on the screen: "You've got to adjust to this world, Gabriel."

"I have adjusted," Mohr typed. "I've adjusted to so many worlds that my head spins. I've adjusted to life on two dozen different clusters, damn it, but I still need my yellow hex!"

He felt uncomfortable having typed this much, and he hadn't revealed anything new. Boursai had already figured out this much about Mohr's past. Mohr thought of breaking the link, but then he thought of the yellow hex Boursai had taken. His only hope of getting it back was convincing Boursai of his need.

"Tell me about that," Boursai prompted.

Nosy bastard, Mohr thought. And then he thought, All right. Maybe — it wasn't likely — but maybe it would even do him some good to write about these things. Some of these things, anyway. There was a lot he would have to leave out.

"If I tell you more, will you return my hex?" he typed.

"I will do what I believe is proper."

"Hell of a guarantee," Mohr wrote, but then he continued: "All right, I'll make you see why I need what I need. And then you'll have to do the right thing."

"That is what I have promised: the right thing."

"When I was young," Mohr typed, "I did some wandering. I started with the Holy Cluster, but I didn't get what I wanted from the Catholics."

Mohr stared at that last word, thinking of the huge, ornate collection of pods and corridors and great rooms that made up the Holy Cluster.

"What were you looking for?"

"You figure it out, Boursai. Anyway, they weren't it. They weren't anything like the believers I had read about in some encyclopedia. The Catholics were so rational that they weren't Godly. They weren't passionate in their beliefs. Their faith was cold and scientific, infected with technologies. It was more psychology than religion. You didn't go to confession to expiate your guilt, as I had read. No, you went to a Process Group to work out your Affective Spiritual Dissonance. God wasn't even in the loop. What mattered in atonement was not that you would make yourself at one with God, but with yourself."

"Faith is tested," came a message from Boursai, "and men speak openly of their doubts. In this way are religions transformed."

"Transformed to the point of meaninglessness," Mohr fired back. Then he froze. He looked back at what he had already written. He was putting down more than he absolutely had to, was feeling more caught up in this than was safe. He had never told his story, the whole story to anyone. But he couldn't just end the transmission, not with his yellow hex hanging in the balance.

He could at least abbreviate what he wrote, not be so detailed. "So I left," he wrote, "and tried elsewhere. I went to the Wahabi Cluster and the Cluster of the All. I tried the Chen Buddhists, the Sikhs, the Baptists and the Bleeders and the Templars of the Void. I lived in the clusters of the Sufis and the Jews. Each time, I held out hope that the answers would be waiting for me at my next destination. Each time, I was disappointed."

"Was your soul unnourished in every place? Did you feel no rumor of God in your heart?"

It was strange that Boursai had put it that way, for that was just the thing Mohr had decided he was looking for: a rumor of God, some whisper of God's voice. A personal revelation. In the face of religions watered down by reason, he wanted direct contact with the divine. He demanded it. Yes, he wanted a rumor of God.

But what he wrote on the com-link was, "God is a lie. But I ran after that lie. I ran to the City of God. For the Citizens of God, God wasn't mere philosophy or a therapeutic tool."

Yes, in the City of God, Mohr remembered, God was still great and absolute and revered. God was God. But He was also a hoax.

Mohr wrote about the City of God haltingly. He didn't really want to remember all of this, but it was the experience that explained his addiction, that would make Boursai return that plastic bag full of oblivion. He thought for a bit, wrote a sentence, thought, and wrote a sentence more.

The first thing the Citizens of God did when he arrived was shoot him full of muscle relaxant and wheel him into surgery. They knocked him out and put a cochlear receiver in his head. All without asking him, almost before they asked him his name.

"The implant," they told him as he came out of surgery, "will teach you obedience to God." And then they taught him the catechism of the Citizens of God while he was still woozy from the drugs.

Obedience was everything to the Citizens — obedience to God's commands. The core of their doctrine was this: God summons each mortal to serve Him, but we are usually so distracted that we hardly hear His voice, and when we do hear, we are too willful to obey. Because of this, God does not call most mortals again, but consigns them to eventual oblivion.

Only those who listen carefully for God's word and prepare to obey Him without thought will know the "release of obedience," the joy of serving a divine master. And so life in the City of God was a continuous drill in servitude.

Several times a day, Mohr would hear a voice in his head, a command spoken directly into his cochlear nerve. In the morning, it would tell him where to report and what to do for the day's labor.

"That part was easy," Mohr wrote for Boursai. "What was difficult was the other half of the day, the evenings in the Hive."

The Hive was a matrix of glass walled rooms in the hub — the weightless center of the City of God. From any room, you could see the six adjacent rooms, and other rooms beyond each of those, stretching on and on until imperfections in the glass made the farthest rooms dissolve into a milky haze.

The voice in Mohr's head would tell him at dinner where he was to report — which cell number. He would undress in his quarters and proceed naked, with all the other Citizens, to his cell. There he would find one or more other Citizens, and the voice would command him again. Sometimes he would be commanded to perform some sex act, or to float at a distance from the other Citizens in the cell, not touching them, not touching himself, while he watched couples or trios in the neighboring cells having sex. Sometimes he was commanded to beat someone. Sometimes he was beaten. Once he was told to push a needle and thread into his palm and draw the thread all the way through his hand. He did it. He'd have done anything. This was the path to God.

"Then one night," Mohr wrote, "I was ordered to beat a man with my fists. Without hesitation, I hit him in the face, time after time. He let himself be bloodied. We would drift toward one another, and then the force of my blow would send us apart. We'd push off from the walls, drift together again, and I'd hit him again. He never raised his hands to stop me. His face was swelling. His lips were split, and the air was red with droplets of blood. I could taste his blood with every breath I took, and the thought came to me that this was madness. So I left the cell. Though the man begged me to go on hitting him, to test his obedience to God, I left the cell."

The wind gusted outside and the walls of Mohr's shelter shook. The wind would stop soon with nightfall. He kept typing: "I went to the elders and I told them that I was going to leave the City of

God, that I was returning to my home cluster of Holdham. But they refused me.

"'You can't stop me,' I told them. 'The laws of the Swarm provide that I may go.'

"And they said, 'What are the laws of men compared to the will of God?' And they told me to return to the hive, to go back and bloody that other Citizen some more."

But he didn't go back. He went to his sack in the dormitory and crawled into it. The voice inside his head ordered him back to the hive, but he refused to get out of the sack. He no longer believed that the City of God could be the path to the divine.

"I refused. They were having none of my apostasy, though," Mohr wrote. "I was trying to escape, but there were a hundred thousand souls in the City, a hundred thousand tools for making me see that escape was impossible. So first, the implant shut up, and then the two biggest men I had ever seen came to the dormitory and beat me while I was still in my bag, beat me until I crawled out and went back to the Hive as they told me to. And in the Hive, they beat me some more. It's strange, but I felt it much more now that I was taking the punishment for punishment alone, not as a step along the path to God. The blows stung as never before."

Mohr stopped for a moment to stare at what he had written. He stared long enough that Boursai queried, "Still there?"

The story was getting closer and closer in time to Tireen. Mohr realized his breathing had become fast and shallow. But if he got the hexes back, they would protect him from the memories he was getting so close to. So he continued, trying to write too fast to think about what he put down: "It wasn't just the beatings. I was used to that. But my whole life in the City changed. The voice stopped speaking to me. I didn't know what to do next, and my actions produced unpredictable results. Whatever I did, some person near me was commanded to do something to me — to give me pleasure or pain, and I would never know which to expect. I would follow the others to work, find a job to do, and try to do it, and some guy would cuff my ear one moment, then pray aloud for me the next. The woman next to me might jab my side with a tool or reach inside my body suit to fondle me. If I enjoyed what she was doing, she might continue or she might bite me. If I stayed in bed, I might get a slap or a kiss. I might be beaten or seduced. I never knew what to expect. I had no control over how people treated me. And so the sight of another human being began to sicken me with anxiety."

He stopped typing and stared at the screen. Was it helping to write these things down? No. Sister Sarah Theresa had been right. A confession had to be spoken aloud. As it was, he was just making himself feel more and more vulnerable. But he still could not turn off the com-link when he thought of what Boursai had and how much he wanted it back.

"You going to give me my hex?"

"Tell me what happened in the City of God."

"They broke me, Boursai. They broke me. When the elders had me carried to their chamber, I begged them to let the voice speak to me again, to order my life once more."

Words on the screen could not say it. They could not represent what had been done to him. For a while he stared at his hands while the wind rattled his shutters and sand hissed against the outer walls of his quarters.

"I see," prompted Boursai.

Not half of it, Mohr thought. He wrote, "People make me sick. All people. I want to be alone. All the time alone."

"But how did you escape them?" Boursai wrote.

"They let me go."

Boursai's reply was long in coming.

"But why? Wouldn't they expect you to go to the authorities, to notify the Court of the Swarm? And haven't you done so?"

"That's my story," Mohr wrote, "or all that matters." He thought of Tireen clawing at his gloved hand, then trying to get her helmet from him. That look. The change in her face, blood boiling under her skin . . .

Writing all of this down was a stupid mistake. Mohr reached into his pocket for a hex.

"Give me my hex," he typed. "It's mine."

Boursai's reply was a question: "Did you ever hear the voice of God?"

Mohr closed his eyes, made no move to reply. When he opened his eyes, there was more from Boursai: "I ask because that is the thing I hope for," the message said. "I hope that one night, when I am on the edge of sleep, God will say to me, 'Momoudu Boursai, there is no God but God. I am He, and Mohammed is my prophet.'"

Mohr typed: "You're a fool. Give me my hex."

"So you never heard the voice of God."

Oh, but he had. He had heard the voice of God all right!

"I heard a voice in my cochlear implant. Not the usual voice. A deeper voice. I was supposed to believe it was God. It told me to go to the Live Free Cluster and make money any way I could. It told me to buy organics and ship them back to the City of God. I

Bruce Holland Rogers

was to enrich the elders, all for the greater glory of God." And now he'd really had enough of this. He had told Boursai all he was going to. "Give me my hex, damn you!"

"Well," Boursai replied, "a message from an imposter does not preclude the existence of God."

Mohr felt flayed open, exposed by what he had written. He was furious with himself for letting Boursai lure him into this exchange. He pounded the keys: "Give me my hex!"

The wind was calming a little, and raindrops sounded on the corrugated roof. It was always like this: strong wind in the early afternoon, then calm, then wind again near sunset and rain at night. The weather on Onazuka's world, a planet with no axial tilt, was as reliable and monotonous as the ventilation cycles in a cluster.

Boursai: "I do not wish for you to suffer."

"My hex, damn it!"

"No matter what the elders did to you, no matter how they broke you down, you are still a human being. You still need other people. Some day, you'll have to come to terms with this."

"Bastard! Thief!"

"You will run out of them eventually. I have the bag before me, now. How long will they last? How will you possibly get more?"

"I need them! I NEED THEM!"

"I will bring them to you. And I will stay away. May you find peace, Gabriel Mohr."

Mohr took a deep breath of relief and turned off the com-link without formally logging off. Then he put his face in his hands and shook. This had been a trial. He felt raw and exposed. But it was worth it if Boursai would now give back his hexes and stay the hell away.

There were, of course, important things that he had left out of the story. He hadn't told Boursai how he had lost his voice. It had no physical cause, his speechlessness. It was his own act of defiance. If God would not speak to Mohr, Mohr would not speak to God. Or to anyone. He would turn his heart and mind to stone.

God had let him search through the clusters, let the corrupt elders break him like an animal, and still God had not whispered one syllable into Mohr's ear, had not dropped one hint, had not said simply, "I am."

The elders in the City of God seemed unsurprised by this loss of speech. Perhaps they were pleased that they had driven Mohr's voice from him. They gave him his wrist communicator.

Mohr also hadn't told Boursai about Tireen, his wife in the City

Wind over Heaven

of God.

Once the elders were convinced that Mohr had been thoroughly conditioned, once they were sure that he thought the new voice in his cochlear implant was truly the voice of God, they assigned him to maintaining the hull of the cluster. Perhaps one day, they told him, if God commanded it, he might be made a missionary, might leave the City of God. But for now his task was to work on the hull, to learn its construction and drill himself on how to repair it should some rare piece of debris come hurtling across the void and strike the home of God's obedient servants.

They gave him a wife, assigned Tireen to him like some cell partner for the Hive.

Mohr went to his door, opened it, and stood listening to the rain. If he'd found wind difficult to adjust to, he had found rain instantly to his liking. He stood outside and felt it fall on his head.

What would Tireen have thought of rain?

And why had he trusted Tireen? She wanted so much for him to trust her, but that should not have been enough. How did he overcome his revulsion, let her touch him? That had been a mistake, letting someone get close to him like that.

She was dangerous, this woman they had given him. She whispered things into his ear, his right ear, for she said that the implant could hear what was said in the left one. She whispered her doubts, her certainty that the City of God was a hoax, a sham that made the elders rich and enslaved the Citizens. She whispered to him her hopes of escaping, of being made missionaries and running away when they had the chance.

Sometimes he was certain that she had been assigned as his wife to trick him, to make him reveal his own doubts and longing to escape. So he did not answer the things she said to him, did not key in any reply on his wrist communicator. But if he was sometimes certain she planned to betray him, he was at other times just as certain that he could trust her, that she meant the things she whispered. But even then he would not answer her with even a glance of encouragement. He was afraid for her. He was afraid that the elders would find out that her faith was pretended, and then they would break her like they had broken him.

But, of course, the thing that had finally happened to her was far worse.

"We must pretend absolute obedience," she whispered in the darkness of their sleeping cell. "Absolute devotion."

As Mohr recalled these things, he found himself taking another yellow hex from his pocket. Hexes numbed him generally, but worked especially on his speech centers. They turned off his inner voice, separated him from memories.

No, he hadn't told Boursai about Tireen, about how he had trusted her so much that one time as he lay in her arms he found himself whispering, uttering words into her ear. He broke his promise to never speak again by telling her that he was with her, that they would escape together, that they would make a life somewhere else and never even remember the City of God. He gave her his word, his spoken word. And she gave him a conspiratorial smile.

And then, an hour later, standing in the airlock together, he looked at her and saw her otherness, saw what a stranger she was. And he was sure, as she helped him to attach his helmet, that she would betray him. She had contrived to make him speak. She would tell the elders that he was not really mute, that he was a blasphemer and spoke of defying them. And the consequences of that? They would return him to the hive. They would try again, try harder than before, to break his will completely.

Mohr he activated the vacuum. The airlock sensors knew that Tireen's helmet wasn't attached to her suit, so he had to hit the override, too.

And Tireen, not believing, did nothing at first. Then she was clawing at his hand on the switch, grappling for her helmet. The expression on her face, before her face was something else altogether . . . the expression of fear and bewilderment. . .

No, he hadn't told Boursai about Tireen. And he hadn't told him, either, why he had taken a handful of yellow hexes and cracked them open, one at a time, inhaling one after another until he could scarcely move, could scarcely remember who he was, but still went on cracking and inhaling. It had been because Boursai had insisted on visiting, had returned time after time to Mohr's compound, no matter how unwelcome Mohr tried to make him feel. It was because Boursai talked and talked about God and the beauty of Onazuka's World and doubt and faith and all the things that Boursai was liable to talk about whether you answered him or not. And Mohr had found himself liking this man. Even as the thought of being within fifty yards of another human being made him queasy, he found himself liking Boursai. And he began to imagine Boursai's face smashed in with a shovel.

Mohr cracked the hex he was holding. There was time enough for one more memory before the hexes covered over his mental past. He remembered the first thing he had felt when he was coming to. The overdose had almost killed him. He had stopped breathing.

And now he remembered the feel of Boursai's breath filling his lungs, breathing him back to life. The man's hot, wet breath. And *that* made him reach for one more hex now to crack between his teeth. And then one more. And then just one more after that.

When he awoke the next morning, the bag of hex was there on the ground outside his door.

‡

In a canyon of blue sandstone, a man is digging a hole. It's a deep hole. It's a grave.

There's a stream flowing nearby. The water is tinted green with algae, an indigenous species. One of the few.

The man digs in silence. There's the sound of the shovel cutting the blue sand. The sound of his breathing. But there's no birdsong. The man is not accustomed to birdsong, anyway, but one day there will be birds in this canyon. And soon, very soon, there will be the buzzing of bees, bees imported from a long way off, light years away, brought here to pollinate the trees. But for now, silence.

‡

At first, Mohr was afraid that Boursai would come visiting in spite of his promise to stay away. For a week, he cracked yellow hex after yellow hex as he constantly scanned the horizon, always expecting Boursai's distant silhouette. But Boursai was a man of his word. When he said he would stay away, he stayed away.

Finally, Mohr tapered off on the hexes and paid attention to his work. He had neglected the trees in his nursery too long, and some of them were dying. He worked hard to get them transplanted and to pamper them once they were in the ground. There wasn't an hour of daylight when he didn't have either his shovel in hand or the water tank on his back. It felt good to work, good to feel the weight of the shovel as he carried it here and there. He worked, in fact, like a man who cared about what he was doing. But what he truly cared about was having something to do that kept his mind from the tiny worm that was eating at his heart.

Sometimes he caught himself gazing in the direction of Boursai's compound, thinking that perhaps he could trust the man enough to tell him about Tireen, to finally poison that worm. To even speak the words aloud. But then he'd think of God, smug and distant, listening, too, to the confession, eavesdropping as Mohr bared his soul. If God existed, God would know already what Mohr had done, but he would not speak of it, not mention it aloud. And whenever Mohr thought of Boursai now, he remembered Boursai's breath filling his lungs, and he'd have to fish a hex from his pocket and crack it in his teeth.

Bruce Holland Rogers

Why did he kill Tireen? That he had suspected her of setting him up, of preparing to betray him, seemed only part of the answer. So he sometimes found himself thinking that thought when his mind was briefly clear of yellow hex. Why did he kill her?

The elders had wanted to know the same thing. Why did you kill her?

"BLASPHEMER," he had keyed onto his wrist.

"Did God command you to kill her?"

He shook his head. "I COULD NOT BEAR THINGS SHE SAID. LIES. BLASPHEMER."

It was easier to lie in writing, much easier than saying the words aloud. And they believed what he said. They made him a missionary to Live Free Cluster, where he was to win, not souls, but wealth. Any way he could, he was to earn money, to buy organics for the City of God. And he obeyed. He stole. He sold his body, repelled though he was by the bodies of others. He did whatever it took to get enough money to keep them happy and to set just a little aside. He bought yellow hex, a lot of it. And when he had enough money he paid a drunken medtech — a real surgeon was beyond his means — to fish out the cochlear implant with a stimwire. That finally shut up the day and night whisperings of the false God in his ear. It was when he was healing from this, unsure if his hearing would return, that the Planters Corps recruiter had found him.

☩

As Boursai continued to stay away, Mohr's life returned to the comfortable rhythm he had known before. He concentrated on getting his trees into the ground and on listening for the hum of the ground skimmer that came to re-supply his nursery. If he could, he would make for the cliffs and hide himself in the canyons until the skimmer crew had unloaded the trees and re-supplied his larder. But if he was too far from the canyons, or if the skimmer surprised him, he would have to endure the conversation, the questions of the crew while he worked alongside them to speed their departure. They would ask him again why they could never reach him on his com-link, and he would key a sentence or two onto his wrist about how the com-link had been down, but he had managed to fix it himself. Or he would say that he had just forgotten to turn it on. And on almost every visit, one of the crew members would ask, "How do you stand it out here? Don't you get lonely?"

Mercifully, such visits were rare, and Mohr could always count on the crew's being in a hurry to finish the day's run and get back to Onazuka City with its closed-in spaces full of people.

Alone again at dusk, he could listen to the rain falling on his metal roof, crack a hex, and drift into silence. No people. No memories. No worm gnawing at his heart.

‡

Then one morning, as he was digging a hole, Mohr heard his name in the still air: "Gabriel!" He looked up to see Boursai striding toward him like some impossibly tall bird, hallooing from the shimmery distance and waving his hand.

Mohr felt in his pocket for a hex.

"I'm sorry," Boursai called out as he drew near. "I'm sorry, Gabriel, but I had to come. There's something I have to tell you about, something I must show you."

Mohr spit the empty yellow shell onto the ground. He held the shovel between himself and Boursai, and he tried to look as unwelcoming as he could.

"If I had a choice, Gabriel, I would stay away. But someone has to know about this. And who else can I tell? Who else can I trust?" Boursai was gesturing wildly as he spoke. Mohr had never seen him in any state but calm and peaceful. Now Boursai moved his arms like some excited stork in a wind storm.

So Mohr keyed the word "WHAT?" onto his wrist, and Boursai stepped close enough to read it.

"You must come with me. Come, and I'll show you."

Boursai was already turning to lead him away, back in the direction of Boursai's compound. Mohr looked at the hole he was digging, at the sapling that needed to go into the ground. Then at his own compound of squatty buildings.

Boursai wasn't waiting for him, nor looking back.

Hell, he thought. He cracked a second hex, breathed in through his teeth, and then ran on his drugged, rubbery legs to catch up. He brought along his shovel. He was so used to having it in his hand that he didn't think of leaving it behind.

It was an hour and a half to Boursai's compound, and they didn't stop there. Boursai kept leading him on toward the cliffs to the west, cliffs much like the ones near Mohr's own compound. There were canyons here, too, Mohr discovered, and Boursai led him into one of these.

What Boursai want to show him was a spring, a six-foot depression in the blue rock. It was ringed with moss that Boursai himself must have planted.

Mohr made a gesture that said something between, "This is it?" and "So what?"

"Look down into it," said Boursai. "Look carefully."

Mohr bent closer to the water. All he could see was a scattering of blue stones at the bottom of the water. What did Boursai expect him to see?

One of the stones moved. Mohr squinted, looked closer.

Again something moved, but now Mohr could see that it wasn't a stone. Mixed in among the stones, blue like the surrounding rock, were a few tentacles or worms of some sort.

"Indigenous life form," Boursai said excitedly, as if he had invented the thing and not merely discovered it.

Mohr nodded slowly and keyed in, "SO?" It was meant to stand for many things: So what? So why bother me about it? So why not just radio it in if it's such a big deal?

"I had to show it to you," Boursai said, "because if I told anyone else, they might try to stop my little experiment." He began to unbutton his fatigues at the collar. "I drank water from this spring before I saw there was something living on the bottom, you see."

He opened his shirt.

Mohr almost spoke. He almost said, "Name of God." Instead, he only mouthed the words and keyed in, "WHAT?"

"I don't know what it is," Boursai answered. He touched the thick, raised welt that stretched across his chest, and something beneath his skin twitched and wriggled. "But whatever it is, it's growing. See this?" He traced what looked like a vein that went from one end of the welt, up his neck, and on to the place where his jaw joined his skull. There it stopped. There was another such vein or filament on the other side of his neck.

Mohr felt his stomach twist, and he dug deep in his pocket for another hex. Cracking it, he keyed in: "GO TO ONAZUKA CITY. GET IT OUT!"

Boursai read the message and said, "No."

"DISEASE!" Mohr keyed in. "PARASITE!"

"No," Boursai said softly. "It's nothing like that. I feel calm, Gabriel, more calm than you can imagine. It's as though . . . Gabriel, it's as though God has touched my mind to tell me to trust this, that this is meant to be."

"CALM," Mohr punched out, "BECAUSE DRUGGING YOU. COMMON IN PARASITES. STRATEGY. PRODUCE TOXINS TO DRUG HOST, BLOCK FEAR, STOP PAIN."

Boursai said, "Perhaps you are right. But then you must look at it this way: what are the chances that a parasite would evolve on this world with a chemistry compatible with mine? Our species evolved light years from one another, beyond contact or influence, so how could we be compatible? How, without the mediation of God?"

"MADNESS," Mohr wrote. "YOURE TAKING TOO BIG RISK."

"It's a miracle, Gabriel. So I'll wait to see what develops. I'll be all right, if that is the will of God. Whatever God wills."

"WHYD YOU BRING ME HERE? WHYD YOU SHOW ME THIS?"

"Why didn't I just use the com-link or write this down in my log? So that someone else has seen the spring. So that there is a witness in case . . . in case it is the will of God that I should die. And also, Gabriel, I had to tell someone. I just had to speak of it. Can a man make a secret of something like this? Can he carry something like this only in his heart? I had to tell someone."

"GO ONAZUKA CITY. GET HELP." Mohr gestured as though he were tearing the thing from his own chest and flinging it away. Then he keyed in, "DIDNT HAVE TO SHOW ME. DAMN YOU!" He let Boursai read this last message, but then picked up his shovel and turned before the man could reply and started to walk out of the canyon.

Damn Boursai. Damn him! he thought. Boursai had given him the burden of a secret, and, damn it, he felt like he had with Tireen, knowing about the things she whispered to him, the blasphemies that were dangerous to both of them. Only this was dangerous only to Boursai himself. No, that made no difference. It was an unfair burden. He didn't want Boursai to die. In spite of everything, his longing to be utterly alone, he didn't want Boursai to die. Not like this. Not with some foul parasite eating away at his flesh . . .

Stop it! he commanded his inner voice. *Shut up!* And he took two yellow hexes from his pocket and cracked them both at the same time.

It was past noon when he got back to his own complex. He went out to where he had been planting the tree, but he just stood looking at the hole, the tree, and then the small, white sun overhead. A breeze tousled his hair. Before long, it would be a wind, and he would want shelter from it. He worked some more on the hole, dug it deeper than it needed to be and put the tree into it. While he packed the sandy soil around the roots, he tried to concentrate on what he was doing, tried not to think.

But it was no good. Thoughts of Boursai, pictures of what he might look like when the thing in his chest was finished with him, kept creeping into his mind. *Damn him!* He threw the shovel to the ground and walked away, leaving the tree only half planted, exposed to the wind. It didn't matter. He didn't care.

God damn that man!

Back in his quarters, he emptied the hexes from all his hidden stashes into the one bag. That at least made his supply look a little bigger. And then he put two more hexes between he teeth. He would shut up the voice inside his head if it took a dozen hexes.

‡

The next day was a little better. He was able to work, at least. But he found himself looking again and again toward Boursai's compound. He was afraid, his guts knotted with fear.

It was like the fear he'd once felt for Tireen.

And damn Boursai once more! Why, when he thought of that man, was he endlessly thinking Tireen?

What would happen to Boursai? How large would the thing in his breast grow to be?

Dig like a machine, Mohr told himself. *Dig. Don't think. Just dig.*

All day he was like that. And the next day, and the day after. He would think of Boursai and of Tireen and he would tell himself to work harder, always harder, until his back ached and his arms shook with fatigue. But he could not resist at some point reaching for a yellow hex, and the first one made it easier to reach for the second.

Finally, he felt he must act. He must do *something*.

He picked up his shovel and set out for Boursai's compound. What he would do when he got there, he was not sure. Was he only going to go to see that Boursai was all right? Or to tell Boursai about Tireen, to burden Boursai as Boursai had burdened him? He didn't know. He just had to go. He shouldered the shovel and walked.

Boursai was not there.

Mohr walked twice around the compound, gingerly opening the doors of the nursery and of Boursai's living quarters. He was not there. Not in the tool shed, not anywhere in sight among the saplings that dotted the land.

He looked toward the canyon mouths that opened in the cliffs. He thought of the spring. Boursai would be there, perhaps, next to the water with the writhing blue things. Doing what? What would Mohr see if he went that way?

Mohr shuddered, imagining Boursai's body covered with twitching welts that hatched, releasing blue worms that wriggled their way back to the water. Or worse. It could be even worse than that, and Boursai would be smiling, drugged by the worms into feeling fine. *Whatever God wills*. What a mistake Boursai was making, to trust the will of God, to trust that *thing* inside his body. To trust anyone or anything at all.

Boursai was going to die. The thing would kill him. That was what came of trusting.

Mohr ran, still carrying the shovel, toward the spring. When he could no longer run, he loped until he could run again. He had brought no water with him. His throat seemed to swell with thirst, but still he hurried on to the mouth of the canyon, into the blue shadows, toward the spring.

When he rounded the corner where he thought the spring was, he thought he Boursai stretched out on the ground, covered all over with blue worms. And he called out, "Boursai!" His voice cracked. "Momoudu!" The sound of his voice echoed back from the canyon walls.

Then he saw that it was not Boursai at all, but only a pile of stones colored a little darker than the ones around them. This was not where the spring was. He had to go further up the canyon.

He wiped the sweat from his forehead and went on. When he found the spring, Boursai was not there.

Mohr sat to catch his breath. He looked at the waters of the spring. Two words, he had called out, the two words of Boursai's name, and his throat was hoarse from shouting. And his throat felt thick with thirst, too, but he would not drink here. Nor from the stream below. He would rather die of thirst.

The blue tentacles waved in the basin of the spring.

Mohr shuddered. He looked around one more time for Boursai, and then he went home.

‡

Eventually, it was Boursai who came to him. It happened late at night, after the winds had died and the rain was only starting. Boursai's voice startled him out of sleep.

"Gabriel," it said again as he lay in the dark, listening. The rain tapped lightly on his roof.

Mohr went to the door without turning on the lights. Boursai was standing away from the buildings, silhouetted against the stars that shone through a break in the clouds.

"I bring you news of paradise," said Boursai. He stood too far away to read Mohr's wrist communicator, so Mohr just stood silently waiting for whatever came next.

The rain continued to fall, tapping on the metal roof and whispering on the ground. The two men stood for a long time in the darkness, listening.

"It is the end of loneliness, this thing I carry in me," Boursai went on. "And you are lonely, aren't you, Gabriel?"

Again there was only the sound of the rain. Boursai lowered himself to the ground. "I hear the voice of a god, now," Boursai said. "Not Allah, not the all-powerful, all-knowing, but an eternal voice. A wise voice. I am never without it." And then he told the story of what the thing in his chest had become.

It was not long after Mohr had come and seen the spring that Boursai began to feel lightheaded and a little ill. Still, he was confident that he had made the proper choice to let the parasite, or whatever it was, continue to grow. In spite of his physical queasiness, he still felt that things were as they were meant to be, that however things turned out, it was the will of God.

The welt was growing thicker by the day, and so were the cords that ran up the sides of his neck. Sometimes Boursai would touch them and feel them throbbing with a pulse that was not his own.

Then one night, he woke with the feeling that someone was watching him. It was no mere uneasiness. This was an almost physical sensation, a certainty that there was another presence with him in the room. In a panic, Boursai switched on the light.

There was no one else in the room, of course. The light shone brightly into every corner, onto the secure latches of the shutters and the door. But even as he assured himself that there was no one else in his quarters, the sensation of being watched did not go away. If anything, it intensified. Was there someone or something outside, peering through a crack in the shutters? No, it was closer than that. There was another being quite near. Inside this room, inside this . . .

Then it dawned on him. Inside his body. There was another mind with him, inside his head.

And with a certainty that defied explanation, Boursai understood that the second mind in his body was discovering the same thing he was: *There is another here. I am supposed to be alone, but there is another.*

Following that thought came this one: *We must go to the water.*

Which meant, of course, the spring.

"So that is what I did, Gabriel. I went to the spring, and the voice inside my head told me to drink. Not by cupping my hands and drawing the water up, but by putting my mouth into the water, drinking like an animal. And when I did this, the thing that was inside me emerged part way . . ."

Mohr stiffened at those words. *How?* he wondered. *Where did it come out?*

". . . and it stretched itself into the water, and the being in the spring reached up to meet it. They touched. They knotted around one another, and they spoke without sound. It was a chemical exchange, I think, one brain trading information with another, and it lasted a long time. I could not rise . . . without pain."

The clouds had closed behind Boursai, so that Mohr could no longer see even his silhouette. He was just a voice floating in the darkness.

"Perhaps I am making you afraid," Boursai said. "You must understand. This is a miracle, a blessing."

And he went on to tell Mohr about the thing that lived in the spring. The blue tentacles were only a small part of it, the tongue-tip of an enormous creature with many mouths, many tongue-tips stretching out to taste the world. Deep below the rock was the main part of its body, winding through the underwater passages of Onazuka's World. From springs here and there, its tentacles emerged to feed, to reproduce, and to communicate. But the being consisted mostly of neurons. It was a huge, ever-lasting mind, and it had been the source of all animal intelligence on the planet before the cataclysm of the meteor.

"The part of it that lives in my breast," Boursai, "is like a remote unit. It has a mind of its own, this thing inside of me, a mind as complex as mine. But when I drank at the spring, it drew upon the intelligence, the knowledge of the greater being beneath the ground. What the greater mind knows, the smaller mind may know by touching it. And so it received an education, this thing inside of me, while I drank at the spring."

The rain fell a little harder now, and the sound of it on the roof was not so gentle.

"PARASITE," Mohr keyed in, but Boursai could not see the glowing letters.

"I carry with me the experiences of a thousand generations," Boursai said. "What each individual mind learns in its life, the great mind receives and remembers."

Again, Mohr thought of the thing emerging somehow from Boursai. Any way that he pictured that happening, it sickened him.

"It thought I was just an animal, Gabriel. It sought to give me a mind, to give me intelligence and direction. But since I already have my own mind, my own volition, it does not struggle with me. It does not command. It asks. It wants me to bring food to the spring, wants me to feed the greater one, which has hungered so long."

"WANTS TO ENSLAVE YOU," Mohr keyed in.

"No it doesn't," Boursai said. He had moved close enough to read the communicator. The hair rose on Mohr's neck.

"I control my body," Boursai went on. "We are two minds in one body. This being is my partner, my companion. Not my master."

Mohr tapped a message out: "WHY DO YOU COME AT NIGHT?"

"Gabriel," answered the voice in the darkness, "this is a miracle. My companion shares my body, shares my life. It knows the wisdom of the ages. Inside my body with me, how can it be my enemy? How can it be anything but a brother to me, a closer brother than any man can be? When it speaks, I feel as though God speaks to me. And I am like the prophet, receiving the holy word, opening my heart."

Again: "WHY DO YOU COME AT NIGHT?"

"I know it is not truly the voice of God, but this thing stands in God's place. Perhaps God speaks to me through it, in some fashion. I am at peace, Gabriel. For me there is no loneliness." Boursai's voice was much nearer now. "Gabriel, there is an end to your fear. There is release from suffering. Come to the spring with me. Come drink at the spring."

"STAY AWAY!" Mohr keyed in.

But the voice came even closer, softened to a whisper in his ear, his right ear, so that he remembered the sound of Tireen's whisper. "All men are brothers, and how much more deeply they may come to know this! Gabriel, I would see you healed!"

For a moment, Mohr was frozen with the memory of Tireen. Then he shook himself and stumbled backward through his door. He turned and made for the light switch by his cot. He tripped, went sprawling.

"I mean you no harm," said the voice outside. "It is up to you, Gabriel. You must choose what you will."

Mohr switched on the lights inside and out. Then he rummaged through his foot locker until he found the hand torch. He went to the doorway, but Boursai was not within the glare of the compound lights. He walked to the edge of the compound and flipped the torch to life. The powerful beam cut through the intensifying rain as he swept it over the flat ground beyond the compound lights. Left, right, in every direction he cast the beam, there was no sign of Boursai.

Mohr walked the perimeter of the compound twice to make sure, directing the light into the shadows of his buildings, the out into the surrounding dark. Boursai was gone.

He went in, took a yellow hex from the bag, and stood looking at it for a moment, reminding himself that he had a choice. He always had the choice of not using. And they were almost gone now. The bag that had looked like an endless supply was almost empty. Maybe, he thought, he should start to ration them. Then he set the shell between his teeth and bit down.

For the rest of that night, Mohr did not sleep. He went from shutter to shutter, to the door, and back to the shutters, checking the latches. Now and then, he cracked another hex.

‡

He needed to do something, but he didn't know what it was. He tried to think about it, tried to decide, while he was in a non-verbal stupor, a haze of yellow hex. As his supply grew smaller and smaller, he grew more and more desperate. But he still didn't know what to do. He tried cutting back on hex, but then there were all of these thoughts and memories flooding in.

He thought of Tireen. He kept seeing his gloved hand on the airlock switch, on the override.

He thought of Boursai, who really did believe that this was a miracle, the thing that had happened to him. And maybe it was. Maybe having that thing living inside your chest, stretching its tendrils into your brain, maybe that was as close as you could ever come to communing with God.

He thought of the worm gnawing at his heart. It twisted and turned inside of him, and he needed to confess, to finally tell someone, anyone, about Tireen. Boursai. He could tell Boursai.

Then he remembered the sensation of Boursai's breath filling his lungs. The hot moisture of Boursai's lips. He remembered how, coming to, he had turned away from Boursai, felt the sandy floor on his cheek, and vomited.

He thought of what it would be like to never be alone again. *Never.*

Thinking these things drove him back to the yellow hexes. He took the last four, and they washed the words from his head. And in that wordless haze, he acted. He shouldered his shovel and walked to Boursai's compound.

‡

Boursai saw him coming from a distance, and he disappeared into his quarters. When Mohr arrived, Boursai had wrapped a cloth about his face so that only his eyes showed. It was afternoon. The wind was blowing and sand was in the air.

"Do you want to come with me to the spring?" Boursai asked.

Mohr nodded.

"Why don't you leave your shovel here?" Boursai said.

Mohr put it down, but felt strange without it. He picked it up again.

"Too used to carrying it?" Boursai said. Mohr could hear the smile in his voice. "Very well. Come."

Bruce Holland Rogers

They walked wordlessly to the spring, but all the time they walked, there was some thought, some urge that was swimming up through Mohr's mind, trying to rise through the fog of yellow hex. There was something he wanted to say, something he wanted to speak aloud. He was grateful for the hex. It kept the words down. At the same time, he could feel it beginning to wear off.

When they arrived, Boursai knelt and gazed into the water. Mohr leaned on his shovel and did the same, peering over Boursai's shoulder. Boursai took a bundle from inside his clothes and unwrapped it. It was grass seed. With a stone and water from the spring, Boursai pounded the seeds into a mealy mass which he then dropped into the water. The blue tentacles squirmed, wrapped around the course dough, and disappeared into the depths of the spring.

"I have so little to give it," Boursai said. "It is hungry. It has had only itself to feed on, eating its own great body, swallowing some of its memories, its wisdom as it did so." He stared into the water where the tentacles were now re-emerging. Then, almost whispering, he said, "Go on, Gabriel. Drink."

Mohr shook his head.

"I thought you came to drink."

Again, Mohr shook his head. A word formed on his lips. A name. *Tireen*. But he made no sound.

"What is it?" said Boursai. "Something is wrong, isn't it?"

Mohr's hands were shaking. The fog of yellow hex was lifting.

"It's the drug, isn't it?" said Boursai. "You've run out."

Mohr nodded.

"We'll talk," Boursai said. "We'll go back to my compound and you can use my com-link. But first . . ." He looked at the spring and began to unwind the cloth from his face. For a moment, however, he paused. "There is a price one must pay for this miracle," he said. He let the last of the cloth drop.

There were slits beneath his eyes, jagged-edged openings with something wet and blue shining from inside.

He dropped the cloth at the edge of the spring. "It is a small price to pay, Gabriel." And he bent toward the water. Blue tendrils slithered from beneath his eyes like snakes, and the tentacles in the water twisted upward to meet them.

"Tireen," Mohr said aloud. Boursai jerked with surprise at the sound of his voice, but he couldn't rise. The tentacles held him in place, and they seemed to keep him from speaking, too.

"There's something . . ." Mohr said. His voice was thick. His whole body was shaking now. The yellow hex had worn off completely. "There's something I . . ."

He felt sick. It was hard to breathe. And how could he say it, what words could he use? "I . . . Tireen . . ." With both hands, he raised the shovel, shaking with frustration. "A thing I did. Didn't mean to . . ." He shut his eyes and felt himself bring the blade down hard on Boursai's neck. Once. Twice. Again and again. He opened his eyes, but kept raising the shovel and bringing it down.

Boursai pulled free of the tentacles for a moment, and the next blow caught him in the face. And the next one.

Mohr didn't stop for a long time. When he did, he said, "Tireen," in an impossibly high voice. He bit his lip and squeezed his eyes shut. It didn't matter what he said now. There was no one to hear him.

There was a tree growing not far up the canyon, a tree that Boursai had planted himself. At its base, Mohr began to dig.

‡

In a canyon of blue sandstone, a man is digging a hole. It's a deep hole, long and narrow. It could hardly be anything other than a grave.

There's a stream flowing nearby. Overhead, the sky is tinted orange with dust, with the color of the setting sun. The wind is blowing hard up there. But down here in the canyon, at the base of these high blue walls, the air hardly stirs.

There is no sound but the soft snick *of the shovel cutting through the sand.*

When the hole is long enough, and wide enough, and deep, the man goes to where the body is. The dead man is tall, his skin black except where it is marked with blood. On his battered face, there are two slits beneath his eyes, and two blue tentacles stretch up from these, twisting and turning in the air. The man raises the shovel and lets it fall again, but the blue worms still twist, still reach for something they can't find in the air.

The man leans on the shovel and is sick.

‡

Why, he wondered as he pulled Boursai into the hole. Why?

Even with his wounds, even with the blue things still waving beneath his eyes, Boursai was beautiful. Why had Mohr killed him?

How could Boursai be dead?

It was the yellow hex, he thought as he shoveled. No, it was seeing him with those parasites in his face, seeing him reduced to a slave, to an animal. Or it was the blue tentacles he wanted to kill, the things that had taken Boursai over?

He filled the trench and scattered the pile of sand that remained. Walking home, he absently reached into his breast pocket, but of course there was nothing there.

‡

His hands shook for a few days, and he sometimes found himself looking in the places where he remembered hiding an extra hex or two even though he had already looked there two or three times before. But that anxiety, that nervous searching, was all that he suffered with the withdrawal. There were no convulsions, no hallucinations, no headaches.

He didn't sleep, but that had another cause. Sister Sarah Theresa's worm of guilt kept him awake, gnawing at his heart.

No. Not one worm. Two.

He would lie awake and think of three things: the air lock, the sound of Boursai's gentle voice, and the thing that still lived in the spring, that abomination, that horror.

To never be alone again, what could be worse than that?

Days passed. Mohr cared for his trees as if in a trance. As he worked, Boursai's face would float into his awareness. Or Tireen's face.

When Mohr slept, it was fitfully. He would wake to hear the sound of Tireen or Boursai whispering into his ear, then would realize it was only the rain.

He hardly ate. Sometimes he would stand under the sun and stare for an hour at the blue cliffs, and finally he began to understand.

He had spoken to each of them. Then he killed. He had broken his pledge to seal his heart from God and from all others.

If he hadn't killed them, who knows what might have come flooding out of his soul? All his fear. All his loneliness. All his longing for God, a God who had sealed His heart against him. Mohr was not worthy of even a divine whisper.

He longed to speak of these things. If only he could tell someone what he had done, and why. He would stand before the com-link an hour at a time, hand trembling on the switch. Then he'd go outside to stare at the blue cliffs, kick at the dust, chew his lip for a while before he returned to hold his hand above the com-link again.

He stopped caring for the trees and they wilted in his nursery, shriveled under the white sun of Onazuka's World.

But if he wrote it down, if he transmitted his confession, what would they do? They would try to help him. They would put him somewhere to watch him, to change him, somewhere close to lots of other people. Bodies all around. Other men breathing the air that he was breathing.

Another man's breath filling his lungs.

The airlock switch.

Boursai lying alongside the trench, eyes half closed and the thing in his chest still throbbing with life.

The twin worms eating at Mohr's heart, digging, burrowing, poisoning his blood.

"When you confess," said Sister Sarah Theresa, "you are poisoning that worm with truth."

He looked one more time, turned the compound inside out. There were no forgotten hiding places, no last stash of yellow hex.

So one afternoon he walked to Boursai's compound, and from there to the spring. He watched the repulsive twisting under the surface. Then he bent toward the water.

☦

It was weeks later that he was lying on his cot, tracing the welt on his chest with his finger. He felt a presence. Some shadow sat at the edge of his mind, looking in on him. He could feel that it was surprised to see him here, astonished to find his head already occupied.

Mohr shuddered. But he tried to ignore the coldness in his gut, the feeling of being flayed open, hopelessly exposed.

It wasn't words that he heard then, but the thought came to him so clearly that it might as well have been spoken. It was an urge, an insistence: We must go back to the water.

The thing inside of him would know his thoughts whether he voiced them or not, but Mohr answered aloud. "I know," he said. His throat felt thick. He did not like the sound of his voice. He coughed and spoke again, "Back to the water. Yes, I know." He felt ill, but he fought the feeling.

The air lock. The shovel.

"But first," Mohr said, "there is something I have to tell you."

An Eye for Acquisitions

Leonard Vriner felt it in his bones, that old magnetic attraction that he hadn't felt in such a very long time. At first he dismissed it. The mergers and acquisitions game as he used to play it was dead, and there just weren't any easy pickings left to be exploited in a corporate raid. But the more he talked to Moscarón, the more sure he felt of the prospect: perhaps there really was one last plum to pluck.

"I can't believe you've never heard of greenmail, Mr. Moscarón," Vriner said to the man he'd just met at the thousand-dollar-a-plate political fundraiser. "Surely, as CEO of . . . What was it again?"

"WWW Service and Supply."

"Yes." Vriner filed the company name securely in his mind. "As CEO, surely you've thought of how you would defend against an unfriendly stock tender?"

"I don't think we'd have a problem."

"Ah," Vriner said, sensing that the plum might not be so ripe. Too bad. "You're closely held."

"Not at all," Moscarón said. "We have no majority shareholders, and our shares trade on the exchange, but our many shareholders want a board and officers who know our business. They are exceptionally loyal."

Vriner was careful not to laugh aloud. How often had he heard that from directors and CEOs? But greed was a persuader that had never failed him. Shareholders could *always* be bought.

"And what does WWW Service and Supply do, exactly?" Vriner asked.

"We are," Moscarón said with a thin smile, "diversified. And becoming more so all the time." The man's eyes were brown with greenish tint, the color of pond scum. "But you were telling me, Mr. Vriner, how you made your fortune. You said you have an eye for acquisitions. Perhaps that's a talent my company can use down the road, when we're a bit more sophisticated."

"My talents aren't for sale," Vriner said, "and I haven't done that sort of deal for a long time."

"Still, it sounds interesting."

But Vriner changed the subject. Why let a naive target know the rules of the game?

And Vriner knew the game well. In the glory days of greenmail and the two-tier tender, in the decade of boardroom bear hugs and bootstrap offers, he had learned the art of the corporate raid. Yes, he did have an eye for acquisitions, a sixth sense for weakling companies that he could buy a taste of and then devour like a shark. Or if he didn't devour, he bit so hard that company's management bid up their own stock to make the deal too pricey, and then he'd sell his stake for a bundle. Win or lose, he made a lot of money. Win or lose, he enjoyed the game.

But the game had changed. The SEC made tougher rules, and companies fought back with self-tenders and the Pac-Man counterbid. Lock-up options and the crown jewel defense kept a company's most profitable divisions out of a raider's reach. There were poison pills and blocking preferreds, staggered boards and golden parachutes and all kinds of other shark repellents. For a while, this had only made the game more challenging, but finally the defense had the edge, and the game wasn't fun any more.

So rather than talk about mergers and acquisitions, Vriner asked Moscarón what he thought of the Senator whose campaign they were supporting at this dinner.

"I've only recently begun to appreciate how useful a Senator can be," Moscarón said.

"You sound as if you own him," Vriner joked. "It takes more than a thousand-dollar dinner to buy a United States Senator."

"Oh, I know that," Moscarón said. "I know exactly what it takes." He took a small box from his vest pocket and opened it. The inside of the lid read, WWWSS. "Would you care for a chocolate?"

"A product of your company?"

"A sideline. As I said, we're diversified."

"I'm allergic to chocolate."

"Pity," said Moscarón.

In the receiving line after the dinner and speech, Vriner noticed that the Senator addressed his contributors by first name, and he glanced into their eyes barely long enough to convey sincerity before he passed on to the next person. "Andy, good to see you. How's business, Leonard? Delighted to have your support. Hi, David, Sheila. Good to see you." But when Moscarón came by, the Senator looked him in the eye long and hard. "Mr. Moscarón," he said soberly. "Good evening, sir. I hope every little thing is satisfactory." And Moscarón just smiled.

Maybe Moscarón *did* own the Senator, and that would suggest that his company had a very healthy cash flow indeed, or else some other attractive leverage that would make the company worth owning.

‡

Vriner called his investment banker that night. "Listen," he said, "I think I've found a Saturday Night Special."

"No way," Siegel told him. "There hasn't been an overnight takeover since dinosaurs roamed the earth. What's your supposed target?"

"WWW Service and Supply."

"Never heard of them," Siegel said. "But I'll take a look. I'll call you soon."

"Call me sooner than soon. I've got a feeling."

‡

In the morning, Siegel paced Vriner's office and said, "Their numbers look sharp, Leonard. But they can't be as unprotected as you say."

"Wide open," Vriner said. "I have it from the head man himself. Now tell me why someone else hasn't gone after them."

Siegel shrugged. "Couple of reasons, I guess. One, maybe no one has *seen* them. It's a low-profile stock, very thinly traded. Weeks go by and no one buys or sells a share. The other thing is that, well, even from their annual report, it's hard to tell exactly what they do. I mean, they trade commodities I can't imagine anyone would want to buy. Cactus spines and live owls. Dried roots and herbs you never heard of."

"And do they do this profitably?"

"They're healthy."

"Let me see."

Vriner flipped through Siegel's report, then passed it back to him. "I wouldn't care if they were cannibals trading in human skulls, Aaron. I like these numbers. Buy me a quiet five percent, and let's go hunting."

‡

Siegel spread the stock trades out over several weeks. Even so, the shares weren't easy to come by. He had to bid the price up to shake loose sellers. "I don't know," he told Vriner. "This is turning into an expensive stake. Maybe they've got wind of you. Making a tender might not be worthwhile."

"I want the deal," Vriner said. "I want to play the game."

"So we go anyway?"

"We go. On Friday, we go."

‡

"It's late, and I'm rather busy," Moscarón said irritably when Vriner called and insisted on an immediate meeting. "Can't this wait until Monday?"

"I think you'd rather talk to me now," Vriner said. "In any case, you have a fiduciary responsibility to hear what I have to say. After all, I have a five percent stake in your company. I believe that makes me one of your largest shareholders, if not *the* largest."

Moscarón sighed. "All right, all right. I'll meet you in my office. You'll have to show yourselves up. My staff is already gone for the day. Do you know how to get here?"

Vriner hung up and smiled at Siegel. "The poor stiff is so out of it that he doesn't know enough to be scared."

‡

"Where in the hell did they get these colors?" Siegel said as he rode the elevator with Vriner. From the outside, the corporate headquarters for WWW Service and Supply had been ordinary enough — blue glass and black steel. The outer lobby, too, was standard and conservative, if surprisingly empty — an open, tiled atrium with a security station absent of security guards. But beyond the public face of WWW, the carpets and wall coverings were sickly shades of green and rust, colors that made the air seem stale and thick. The inside of the elevator was the color of bread mold.

"That'll be the second thing that I get rid of," Vriner said, tapping the elevator wall.

"The first, presumably, is Moscarón."

"I'm not going to have someone so simple-minded running any company of mine."

"He does seem to have a Senator in his pocket, from what you say."

"Anybody who's rich enough can do that if he cares to."

"Don't kid yourself."

Moscarón's office was on the top floor, but it was hardly what Vriner expected in an executive suite. Flames flickered in the fireplace near Moscarón's desk, and the room was stuffy with stale smoke — not wood smoke, but something more rancid, like the smoke from burnt hair. The fluorescent lights seemed ordinary enough, but they cast a dim light that didn't quite illuminate the corners of the expansive room.

"My time is short," Moscarón said. "Come, sit, and tell me what

Bruce Holland Rogers

this is about."

"What this is about," said Vriner, staying on his feet as Siegel sat down, "is my holding company's offer for a controlling share of WWW Service and Supply. I told you I have an eye for acquisitions, Moscarón. I also have a pretty good idea of what constitutes an irresistible price. We're buying you out at thirty-two dollars a share."

"I see," Moscarón said. "Well, it's out of the question. The company is not for sale."

"We'll see what your shareholders have to say about that. I want you to produce, by tomorrow, a list of your owners."

"This company's shareholders," Moscarón said, "are very private people. I'm sure they don't want me passing out their names and addresses to anyone who asks. Now I have things to do tonight. You will excuse me."

Vriner laughed, and Siegel said, "You have a fiduciary responsibility to your shareholders to let us make our offer known to them. Failure to live up to that responsibility will land you in civil court."

"I'm a shareholder, too," Vriner said. "My interests are your interests. Or they had better be."

Moscarón shook his head. "I don't want a court battle just now. I haven't made arrangements for that sort of thing. But I don't think you understand who you are dealing with. You say, Mr. Vriner, that you have an eye for acquisitions. Perhaps you do. But in this case, your eye has misled you. Our shareholders . . ."

Something moved in the dark corner behind Moscarón.

"What's that?" said Siegel.

"An owl," Moscarón said, and Vriner could now see it in the shadows, a small owl on a tall perch. Its eyes glinted from the darkness.

"I don't want excuses," Vriner told Moscarón. "I want that list tomorrow."

"All right," said Moscarón. "You'll have your list." He opened a confection box and pushed it toward Siegel. "Would you care to try one of these?"

"We're taking over your company and you're offering us chocolates?" Vriner said.

"You might as well know something about what you're trying to take over."

Vriner waved off the offer, but Siegel accepted.

On their way out of the building, Vriner said, "You see what I mean about this guy? He just doesn't get it."

Siegel didn't answer. He was fishing around in his mouth with his tongue, and finally he gagged and reached in with his fingers. He drew out a long, long black hair. Tied to the end of it was a wet little bundle that looked like animal fur.

Siegel had the dry heaves there in the empty hallway.

"Was that in the chocolate?" Vriner said, looking at the glistening hair.

"Must have been," said the investment banker, getting his breath. "You might be buying yourself a huge consumer product liability suit, Leonard, if that's a standard ingredient." Siegel retched again and spit into his handkerchief.

"Maybe that's Moscarón's idea of a takeover defense," Vriner said with a smile. "Nauseate the opposition."

"You still want to buy a company that makes chocolate with hair in it?"

"I want a deal, Aaron. I'm hungry for a deal."

‡

"No one's selling," Siegel reported over the phone a week after the offer had been tendered.

"Aaron," said Vriner, reclining behind his desk, "we're bidding five dollars above the last trade."

"Yeah, but that last trade was a week ago. There's no movement. I can't even get anyone to report an asking price. It's as if we've already bought up all the shares that are going to be sold."

"Out of ten thousand shareholders spread out all over the world, out of all these penny-ante owners, you can't squeeze even a handful of shares?"

"Can't squeeze *one* share. It's like the word is out that the stock will be worth a million a share tomorrow, you know?"

"No, I don't know. This doesn't happen. People get greedy."

"I can't figure it, either, Leonard, but I'm getting bids to buy back your stake at a little bit under what you paid for it. I think maybe it's time to cut your losses and run."

"I don't run."

"Well, maybe you do this time, if you're smart. Your own stock is trading at record volume. There may be a move afoot to cut your feet out from under you."

Vriner sat up. "Moscarón?"

"I'm having Erlich & Bahr look into it. So far, the orders are spread between a dozen street names, so if it's one buyer, he's doing a hell of a job of disguising himself."

"I didn't think the old boy had it in him," Vriner said, grinning, relishing a fight.

"Don't take this lightly," Siegel said. "You're heavily defended,

Bruce Holland Rogers

but there's a lot of capital moving your shares. If this is Moscarón, he has heavy hitters backing him."

"I'm going to put Logan Edwards on this. He can do a background check on Moscarón, and I'll have him check out some of the shareholders, too."

"That's going to get into some money. Ninety percent of the shareholders are overseas."

"I don't care. I want to know who these people are. What's their compelling interest in maintaining control? With a little insight, Aaron, we can still break this open."

"You're the boss, Leonard. Listen, though. I'm going to orchestrate this from bed for a day or two. I don't feel so hot. Touch of flu, maybe."

"I need you on this, Aaron."

"Have I ever let you down?"

‡

In wing tips, a business suit and neck tie, Logan Edwards didn't look much like a gumshoe. On the other hand, he wasn't the usual sort of private investigator.

"I've pushed it hard," Edwards said, looking from Vriner to Siegel. "I've got six of my best people digging full-time into Moscarón, and we can't get much. I can tell you that he's been in New York for ten years, has been CEO of WWWSS since incorporation, and was in Gallup, New Mexico, before that. But I've had a hell of a time finding anyone who knew him, and those who did know him won't talk at any price. They're spooked, I think." Then to Siegel, Edwards said, "You don't look so good."

"No," Siegel said, blinking his red-rimmed eyes. "I don't feel so hot, either."

Vriner wanted to stay with business. "Mob connections?"

"Could be," Edwards said, "but I doubt it. There's not enough in Gallup to get the attention of organized crime."

"What about the shareholders? You've done background checks on them as well?"

"I've run into brick walls," Edwards said. "It's the same story over and over. You wouldn't believe the places where holders of small lots live. Tiny villages in Africa and South America. On the other hand, you've got big industrialists in Germany and Spain, people of Moscarón's stature and much bigger, and all of them are as opaque as can be. If my people meet them, they won't talk, and their neighbors won't talk. I can't get squat."

"For three million dollars, that's what you give me? Less than squat?"

Edwards held up his hands in a gesture of helplessness. "I'm as frustrated as you are, Mr. Vriner."

"Not yet, you aren't, Edwards. From now on, you're off retainer. Get out of my office."

Edwards stood.

"Don't do this," Siegel said feebly. "Logan is the best in the business."

"The best investigator in the business," Vriner said, "would bring me useful information about my opponent. For that matter, the best *investment banker* in the business, which you used to be, would be finding his own ways to stop Moscarón."

"Short of a self-tender," Siegel said, "what can we do? We know this is a tidal-wave open-market assault by a whole bunch of coordinated buyers."

"Don't hand me excuses," Vriner said. "Give me results!"

‡

But things got worse. Two loyal members of Vriner's board of directors died of sudden illnesses, and another, Greg McCarthy, moved to call an emergency meeting to rewrite the corporate charter.

"Rewrite it for *what*?" Vriner said.

"To rescind your golden parachute, Leonard. I think it's pretty much unanimous that we're a company with hardened arteries."

"You can't dump me! I'll sue your ass!" Then, more gently and reasonably, Vriner said, "I founded this company, Greg."

"Things change," McCarthy told him.

‡

Moscarón wouldn't answer his phone. Time after time, Vriner would call WWWSS, talk to a receptionist, and then be transferred to a phone that rang forever. Vriner thought of leaving a message, but that would put the ball in Moscarón's court. He decided to see the man in person, to catch him off guard if possible, though he wasn't sure of exactly what his approach would be if he could get through to him. Negotiate a compromise? Beg for mercy?

He went in the early evening when shadows were lengthening and the streetlights were coming on. As before, the lobby of WWW Service and Supply was empty.

Vriner took the elevator up. There was no receptionist in the outer office. The door to Moscarón's inner sanctum was unlocked.

A fire crackled in the fireplace, and the room again smelled of a sickly smoke. Moscarón was nowhere to be seen.

A shadow moved in the corner — the owl on its perch. Vriner steeped towards it for a closer look. The owl turned at the sound

Bruce Holland Rogers

of his approach, and Vriner squinted into the dark to see it better. There was something strange about the animal, but it the half light, it was hard to say exactly—

Vriner stepped back.

The bird had no eyes. Where its eyes should have been, there were only empty sockets.

Vriner turned away from Moscarón's repulsive pet, and when he did, he saw the yellowed orbs that sat in a dish on Moscarón's desk.

There was no mistaking them, or what they came from.

They were eyes. Human eyes the color of pond scum, turned up on the dish so that they seemed to be looking at him.

What he did next wasn't rational, and even as he did it, Vriner knew that he should probably leave the things alone. But he wanted them out of his sight, out of his *memory*. Retching, Vriner picked up the dish and carried the eyes to the fire. He threw them in and heard them pop and hiss in the flames.

‡

Moscarón's call came the next morning. "I'd like to come by for a chat with you and your banker," he said. "Say at three?"

"Siegel's here with me now," Vriner said. "Why don't you come and get it over with."

"All right," Moscarón said. "Why not?"

Vriner hung up. "He's coming," he said.

Siegel — eyes rheumy, face pale — nodded. "At least it will be over soon, Leonard."

Vriner closed his eyes. It would, in fact, be almost a relief.

‡

When the receptionist showed him to the office, Moscarón started to come through, but then bumped his shoulder against the doorjamb.

"Are you all right?" the receptionist said, not knowing the enemy when she saw him.

"Fine, fine." Moscarón was wearing sunglasses. "You can leave us," he said, as if she already worked for him.

The receptionist closed the door on her way out, and Moscarón approached Vriner's desk somewhat hesitantly, groping for the chair when he was still a foot away from it. Siegel got up and helped him. Moscarón sat down heavily, as though grateful to quit navigating through the office.

"Well," Moscarón said to Vriner, "I have certainly learned a lot from you." He reached into his pocket and put what looked like a silver soup spoon on Vriner's desk. The handle was engraved with WWWSS.

"What's that?" Vriner said.

"An item from our catalogue."

"I didn't know there was a catalogue."

"As I told you when we met," Moscarón said, smiling from behind the sunglasses, "we are a diversified company. But the catalogue does not circulate widely."

"Why don't you cut the crap," Vriner said, "and tell me that you're here to tender an unfriendly offer for control of my company."

"I hardly need to do that," Moscarón told him. "My associates already hold a majority interest in Vriner Holdings, but in many small bites. We prefer to be subtle. No SEC filings and disclosures this way. My associates are very private people."

"So I've learned."

"Have you?" Moscarón said. "I still don't think you understand who we are." Then, to Siegel, Moscarón said, "Show him, Aaron."

Vriner looked at Siegel. Who was taking something out of a black case. "Aaron? You're working both sides?"

"Only temporarily," Siegel said. "After today, my services go exclusively to Mr. Moscarón."

"I'll sue your ass into kingdom come," Vriner said, sitting up straight, sensing that all might not be lost after all.

"No you won't," Siegel said, and with a deft movement, he flicked gray powder from the case into Vriner's face.

"What the hell—" Vriner started to say, but Moscarón uttered a syllable and Vriner froze in mid-sentence. He could see, he could hear, but he could not speak or move.

"Nicely done," said Moscarón. "I thank you. My current condition has naturally done nothing for my aim."

"All right," Siegel said. "He's yours. Now help me."

"I always fulfill my obligations, but I would thank you to speak more respectfully."

Siegel lowered his head. "Yes, Mr. Moscarón. Of course, Mr. Moscarón."

"Open your mouth."

Still unable to move, or even to look away, Vriner watched as Moscarón coiled a long hair onto Siegel's tongue.

"Swallow," he said, still holding one end of the hair.

Siegel obeyed, and Moscarón uttered another syllable, then began to pull gently on the hair.

Siegel gagged. "Easy, now," Moscarón said.

A black mouse, squirming and covered with slime, erupted from Siegel's mouth. The banker turned and vomited.

Bruce Holland Rogers

"Please!" Moscarón said. "Not on the carpet!"

Siegel stayed doubled-over, catching his breath.

"You understand," Moscarón said, "that there are others. You'll be fine for a while, but if you don't come to me as they mature, they'll fill your body. To the uninitiated, it will look like cancer."

"I understand," Siegel said, wiping his brow. Already he looked better. "You have my unquestioned loyalty, Mr. Moscarón."

Moscarón turned toward Vriner. "Ah, Mr. Vriner," he said. "How very helpful you have been to World-Wide Witchcraft Service and Supply."

He sat down again, as if the business meeting were to continue.

"You've taught us a lot, sir. You've done a great deal to show us the way. Between a good investment banker and a few hundred coordinated witches, I don't think there's a company in the world that can resist us."

He stood again and leaned toward Vriner with the mouse. Something wriggled through Vriner's lips, and then Vriner felt Moscarón's fingers push the mouse past his tongue. It squirmed down.

Moscarón took off his glasses. Black and yellow eyes no bigger than large marbles rolled in his eye sockets.

"Unfortunately, your little visit while I was out conducting some night business deprived me of an important asset."

He picked up the spoon.

"We have a lot of advantages in a corporate environment," Moscarón said. "Who, in the boardroom, believes in witches? Who knows how to mount a defense against us?"

He leaned forward, and one of the owl eyes almost rolled out of his head.

"But I can't very well do business looking like this, can I? I think suspicions might arise. Agreed?"

Deep in his stomach, Vriner felt tiny teeth beginning to gnaw. He'd scarcely have believed that something so small could cause so much pain.

"You say you have an eye for acquisitions."

Moscarón slid the edge of the spoon beneath Vriner's eyelid. If Leonard Vriner hadn't been frozen into silence, he would have screamed.

"I wonder," Moscarón said, "which one it is?"

Cloud Stalking Mice

Rev. John J. Tiller
Baker City, Oregon
Eighth of September 1899

Rev. W. C. Harris
Oregon City, Oregon

My dear brother in Christ,
   You have inquired about my health, and I confess that I am not well. Mary will scarcely let me out of the house except to conduct services. Walking exhausts me, and she says that my face goes purple when I have done no more than cross the room to poke the fire. Long gone are the days when I could count the miles of wilderness walked as well as the scores of souls saved. There are not many miles left in these legs. Even my days as pastor of this church cannot number very greatly.
   Bishop Golden was present in Baker City for the Sabbath just past, and he told my congregation that they were fortunate to walk alongside me as I took my last steps toward Home. "There are no heroes like the heroes of the cross," he said, "and no pioneers like the pioneers who brought salvation into the wilderness."
   I hope that my flock took comfort in those words. As for me, I find myself without the sure consolation I once had. I do have a cat. He sits upon my lap as I pen these words, and his purring comforts me more than anything the bishop might say. But he is an earthly comfort, and therefore wanting.
   I am in despair, William, for the sake of justice.
   There are two puzzles that I recently sought to solve. In the first instance, I revealed a murderer. In the second instance, I wrestled

with a celestial mystery, one that I had rather left unexamined. Its unwinding has been like the unraveling of a garment that once warmed me.

Were you here, I know that you would demand to know the particulars of my desolation. Then you would endeavor to apply chapter and verse to the wound, and by the Word, heal me. But William, it is by the Word that I am wounded. Raised up, yes, saved from the eternal grave, yes, but wounded also.

This despair of mine has come in stages. In stages, then, will I relate it.

I.

You know that I held camp meetings at the Klamath Indian Mission some years ago, but I do not think I ever spoke to you of the experience. From a rude pulpit erected under the pine trees, I held services for some eight hundred red men and women. A Christian Indian was my interpreter. I took as my text the Decalogue, laying God's law before them. I emphasized the "Six days shalt thou labor," for Indian men are especially prone to idleness. I told them also that many white people were not Christians because they themselves were too lazy. I then commenced to unfold for them the Day of Judgment, to describe its terrors. All of this was conveyed with great effectiveness by my interpreter.

In any camp meeting, I have always felt an exultation when, calling all who desired to become Christians to come forward, I should find large numbers prostrate before me and crying for God's mercy. Yet how much more it meant to me when the Indians' petitions to our Father were answered by their conversions. How they rejoiced, these simple children of nature! Over one hundred were baptized on that first occasion.

I was never seized with the conviction that I ought to go as a missionary to Africa, but my experience with the Indians did produce a similar conviction that I must strive to Christianize the colored races whenever I encountered them in Oregon.

Thus it should not surprise you to learn that when the last Conference appointed me pastor to this Baker City church, I proceeded to study the Chinese residents of the town. There had once been a great many of them here to build the railroad, and no small number remained as prospectors or laborers. Now there were more white settlers here than previously, and the Chinese were not so much needed for their labor. Such is no doubt the case in all of Oregon, and in the whole of the country, since the law will not permit more of them to enter. By the time I had come to Baker

City, many had already returned to China. The rest were expected to return before too long. If I could effect conversions among them, this might effectively be my missionary work to China, for they would take the Gospel with them on their journey home.

But the obstacles to their conversion were considerable. I spoke not a word of Chinese, and most of them spoke English but poorly. Also, my experience among the Klamath had taught me how necessary is the lever of a first conversion. My interpreter did more than reshape my words to the Indian tongue. He demonstrated by the example of himself that an Indian could live by God's laws and know salvation.

For the object of my ministrations I chose a Chinaman called Kong-Cheong. He suited my purposes well on both counts. First, he had learned to read, write, and speak clear English. Second, he was a doctor to the Chinese, well respected among them. If I could bring him to Christ, I was assured that many other Chinese would follow.

I first went out to his cabin to engage him in conversation and ascertain what he knew of scripture. It was the springtime, and Baker City's streets were thawing to mud. The slope I must climb outside the town was much the same. My boots were heavy with muck and pine needles by the time I reached the stand of trees where the Chinaman's cabin stood. Though I had come slowly, the effort had exhausted me. I labored like a bellows to get enough air.

There was yet a chill to the days, so I was surprised to find the cabin door standing open. No sooner did I arrive at the doorway than Kong appeared in his quilted jacket. Before I had caught my breath to make my introduction, he took me by the elbow and peered up into my face. After a solemn moment, he said, "Too much heat. Your heart, I think it is." Then he leaned forward, as if to listen to my wheezing or smell my breath. Taking my wrist, he felt my pulse for some moments. "Yes," he concluded, "it is certainly your heart."

This made a curious greeting and introduction. All the more surprising, his diagnosis agreed with that of my own white doctor.

"For this," the Chinaman continued, "you must encourage the kidneys. Kidneys rule the heart, and water cools the fire. Come in. Come in." He led me to a rough bench where he bade me sit down. Bending over a table at the back of his cabin, he asked me questions. How often did I pass water? Did I often eat salty foods? Bitter? Pungent?

He began to advise me as to changes in my diet while he assembled dried plants from which I was to brew an infusion. Only when he went to write in his ledger did he ask my name. Without any conscious decision to do so, I had become one of Kong-Cheong's patients.

"I am of meager means," I told him, "and barely able to afford the physician I already have."

"Do not worry for that," he said. "Pay when you can."

I remembered my purpose enough to ask him what he knew of God and holy scripture. He gave me a curious answer. "Look there," he said, pointing to a corner where a white cat lay napping. The animal was tethered by a length of string to a table leg, as was the custom among the Chinese. "There is all the book a wise man needs."

"The cat?"

"Or as easy a bird could be the book. Or a stone."

I thought perhaps some misunderstanding of speech would explain his remarks. "I am speaking of a special book," I said. "I mean the Bible, God's word."

"Words are written in all things," he answered. He brought out a stool and sat before me. "How can one separate a maker from what is made? How would you know your God if you do not look all around?"

"By His word, the Holy Bible," I said, "which is His revelation."

"Perhaps it is," Mr. Kong said. "So is my cat a revelation."

I detected no impiety in his manner and perceived that we had entered into a debate. I decided that we had made a promising start, and I launched from that beginning to an explanation of sin and redemption. I told him of the terrors of judgment and of the personal salvation he could enjoy in Christ. He listened. I could not have misread the interest written upon his face. But at the end he said, "Good and bad are like this: No man is all saved or all damned. Everyone is some of each. How can you separate the sun side of a mountain from the shadow side?"

Pleased to think of so apt an answer and feeling the influence of the Holy Spirit in my words, I said, "The light of Christ shines on both sides of your mountain. By Him is the shade made glorious light."

"Then the shadows are beneath," Kong said, shaking his head. "All aspects are two." In that same moment, I found that Kong's cat was staring at me. The fixity of the animal's green gaze unnerved me.

I looked away from the animal. As I thought of what answer to give Kong-Cheong, he said, "Forgive me, Mr. Reverend Tiller. I must go today to see the son of Mr. Halbower, and then I have

Bruce Holland Rogers

appointments in Sumpter. Come tomorrow, if you wish. Early. Do not neglect to take tea, three times. Drink water. We must give your kidneys strength to cool the heart." Then he ushered me to the door.

II.

Although I have been blessed with good results in leading camp revivals, I confess that such revivals were not my favorite means for winning souls. I am sorry to see the Conference lately preferring the public shout of revivals to the close whisper of class-meetings. That many are saved at a camp meeting I know very well, but of those many converts, how many will be lost again at the first shadow of doubt? In class-meetings with a few wayward souls, the preacher is better able to show the road and the converts are better able to keep it. One whose step falters will more readily find a Christian hand to steady him in the class-meeting.

More than that. I miss the class-meeting for the nearness of the sinners I would save. Class-meetings were conversations. Revivals are exhortation only. In short, I miss knowing so well the souls I endeavored to bring to God.

I tell you this to explain why I found myself going almost every day to the Chinaman's little cabin. Our conversations recalled the satisfactions of my early ministry, at least in form. In substance, I was much more successful even in my earliest, most awkward attempts to preach the gospel than I was in my efforts to convert Kong-Cheong.

Chief among his beliefs was the dual nature of things. Light he twinned with darkness, damp with dry, hot with cold, and if I am not mistaken, good with wickedness. In this last matter, he was not inclined to give direct answers to my inquiries. "A man should serve as it is his place to serve," he might say, or "Rain is good for the earth, but the fire does not love it." His medical opinions ran to the same dualities: too much damp injured the spleen, too much dryness injured the kidneys. When I turned our conversations to the Deity, Kong would sometimes suck on his little pipe and say only, "That is all," by which he meant I know not what. My efforts to draw him out on the matter produced strange questions. Why was it necessary for God to precede creation? Weren't they the same thing?

Most assuredly they were not! I gave him Genesis, but this moved him not at all. He seemed little moved by any words of scripture, or by any proof I gave him that the Bible was God's true word and covenant.

Wind over Heaven

At another time in my life, I might have given up and taken the seed of my evangelism to more fertile ground. Now, however, I made myself fast to Kong's cause. I reminded myself that making a Christian of this man could be a first step in the salvation of countless Chinese souls. And as I have said, I enjoyed our conversations as if they were class-meetings. Besides, I was supernumerary in my service to the Baker City church. My duties were light and left me time to pursue Kong's salvation without fear that my attentions were needed somewhere else.

Kong's medical attentions coincided with God's mercy, and I began to recover my health. I drank the teas he prescribed for me and did certain exercises he taught: swinging my arms a certain way, rubbing my kidneys, describing circles with my hands and suchlike. I did them indoors. Kong said I must have fresh air as I practiced his "chee gong," but Mary overruled, declaring such an out-of-doors display unseemly. Though my physician in Baker City doubted the efficacy of the Chinaman's medicines, he did pronounce me much improved.

Kong and I traded other talk. He extracted from me tales of my life as an Idaho miner and the story of that Cayuse Indian who saved me in a snowstorm. From him I had stories of his family and the famines in China. He told me, too, of his various patients, Chinese and white, and the puzzles their ailments provided. For poisoned blood, ranchers and miners were more apt to call on Kong than on the white doctors in Sumpter or Baker City. Kong often cured it, and he never amputated. Furthermore, he practiced by mail when he could not travel to his patients and they were too ill to come to him. They would describe their symptoms in a letter, and he would send medicine by return post. "That is not best," he told me of prescribing without an examination, "but sometimes it is necessary."

I learned, too, that the name of his white cat was Cloud Stalking Mice. "He moves like this," Kong said, moving his own shoulders in slow circles, stopping, moving again. "He teaches me a new chee gong, I think."

With the arrival of summer, Kong and I moved our discussions outside, sitting in the shade of pine trees. The Chinaman sometimes tied a weight around his cat's neck and brought him out with us, trusting the encumbrance to keep Cloud from roaming far. In China, he explained, not even the male cats strayed from home. They were too useful to lose. He was surprised that cats were not similarly treasured here.

Kong's conversion still did not progress. I had much hope for him, as he was a deliberate and thoughtful man. But that frustrated hope produced in me a state of growing agitation and despair. How often have we seen it that some sinner hesitates in the question of faith, then of a sudden dies before he is enlisted with Christ? My passion to save Kong grew stronger. More than Christian duty moved me. I began to fear for him as I would for a friend.

III.

One day as Kong and I sat talking beneath the pines, three black-tailed does made their way from the brush into the clear. We paused in our conversation to watch them as they browsed. They took no particular notice of us nor of the white cat resting at Kong's feet. At first.

Then Cloud roused himself, stretched from tongue to tail, and walked lazily toward the cabin, which brought him, as if by coincidence, nearer to the deer. The does raised their heads to watch him, them recommenced their browsing. The cat seemed not at all interested in them, and they were not interested in the cat.

But as he neared the cabin and had the cover of some brush between him and the deer, a change came over Cloud Stalking Mice. He lowered his body so close to the ground that the weight tied to his neck dragged across the fallen pine needles. With his gaze fixed on the does, he crept slowly toward them. Little vibrations shook his body and were exaggerated in his tail.

This change in the cat did not go unnoticed by the deer. All three raised their heads. Their noses twitched, and the legs of all three began ever so slightly to tremble. They knew they were being stalked. The creature that had seemed unimportant to them a moment ago was now terrible to them.

Cloud Stalking Deer crept forward just an inch more, and the does bolted. I laughed and admitted my surprise that the deer would perceive Kong's little mouser a threat to them.

Kong did not laugh. He sucked on his pipe, then said, "There is a lesson in the affairs of men," he said, "and perhaps in the ways of heaven as well."

I asked what he could mean by this, and he answered that he did not know, that he would have to ponder the matter.

IV.

One of Kong's neighbors was a man known by the name of J. T. Smith, or Old Smith. I had never seen the fellow, though I knew of him from the speculative talk in town. He was very jealous of trespassers and was liable to meet them with rifle in hand, eager to educate them upon the matter of his property rights.

Smith's notion of those rights did not correspond with any recorded deed. Nor had he registered a mining claim, though some of the speculation about him conjectured a small deposit of gold on "his" property since he occasionally bought supplies with the yellow dust. Such a mine was unlikely. There was no stream through Smith's territory, nor any water except what could be drawn from a well, and a man cannot work a deposit without plentiful water.

It was supposed by some that Smith earned his gold from miners at Sumpter. They came to Baker City sometimes for supplies, owing to the high price in Sumpter. But if Old Smith rendered them some service, none of them ever spoke to reveal its nature.

I chanced to be present when Smith presented himself and his rifle at the doorway of Kong's cabin. At first, I did not know who he was, this big white-bearded man who had stumbled in upon us. Gray locks lay matted against his sweaty forehead. His face was bright red. I perceived a pistol worn on his hip. But then I guessed his identity.

Smith seemed hardly to notice I was there. He pointed his rifle at Kong and said, "I need doctoring."

Kong regarded the gun with calm. "Better you don't shoot me if you need a doctor," he said.

"Just you get me some medicine," Smith said. "I got the bad chills." His hands trembled. "Understand? You give me medicine plenty hurry. You plenty hurry, Chinaman. You plenty hurry or you plenty sorry."

At this point I interjected my opinion that Mr. Smith should sit down and submit himself to Kong's examination. Smith swung the gun in my direction and said, "What I got is the *chills*. I know better than him what I got!" But at last he did sit down and permit Kong to take his pulses and give him a tea to drink.

In the end, Kong and I both helped Smith back to his cabin where he became delirious with his fever, alternately thanking and berating Kong and sometimes seeming to speak to persons not actually present. The cabin was an arsenal, containing an additional rifle, a shotgun, and a derringer upon Smith's rough night table. Skins and feathers testified to Smith's success as a hunter, and I wondered if he might not simply earn his mysterious gold by this means.

As night approached, Kong stayed to attend to Smith while I returned to Baker City. Smith apparently recovered his health, for in the following weeks, Kong said nothing about him.

V.

My acquaintance with Kong-Cheong might have long continued, even unto his eventual conversion, save for the intervention of just such unhappy circumstance as I might have feared. By which I mean to say that he was murdered.

I learned of his death from the Chinaman who brought me Kong's cat. In sentences of one or two words, he conveyed to me the news of Kong's killing and made me understand that Kong had desired me to have Cloud. I do not know when or how Kong had communicated this wish. Perhaps the Chinese who saw to his affairs had found none among their number who would take the cat. At any rate, Kong's killing made Cloud Stalking Mice my inheritance and remembrance.

The murder of Chinamen is not common here, but it happens more frequently than the assassination of white men. The Chinese of Baker City know that to be found on the streets after dark is to invite the sport of cowboys and other rough fellows. And there have been a few massacres which you may recall. Some years ago, seven men killed a score of Chinese miners on the Snake River and took their gold.

Watching the cat, who returned my gaze with his own strange stare, I reflected on my failings. Kong-Cheong had died unredeemed when I might perhaps have been less conversational and more exhortative in my efforts for him. I pondered also the wickedness of my fellow men, that we should shoot dead one of our yellow brethren who was a gentle healer, and just when he was first becoming acquainted with the gospel! The injustice of it gnawed at my brain. I could not cease from brooding upon the matter. I even made inquiries of the sheriff, who could tell me only that Kong had been shot twice in the back of the head outside of his own cabin and that the identity of his killer was unknown. He expressed the opinion that the Chinese often settled their differences among themselves and that the killer might never be known.

Again I remind you, William, as I wish I had reminded myself, that earthly judgment is not properly our task. Yet I thought I must do something for Kong. I must make some gesture in his memory. I determined, after my interview with the sheriff, that I would myself find the killer out.

VI.

I conceived a theory regarding the murder. I knew that Kong carried some of his patients on credit, for he had done so with me.

Wind over Heaven

Thus, a patient owing a substantial sum might have a motive for erasing his debt. From the Chinaman who had brought me Kong's cat, I secured an accounting from Kong's ledger, showing what debts were owed, and by whom.

Interviewing former patients, both Chinese and white, was the work of some days. Kong's practice, and the debts owed to him, were widespread. But the miles I must walk seemed to strengthen, rather than exhaust me.

I continued to take the tea which Kong had prescribed for me, and I began to practice my "chee gong" exercises just as he'd told me to, out of doors, in fresh air. Mary protested daily that the neighbors must think me very queer. But I persisted.

In the course of my investigation, I met a Belgian miner called Heuse who had suffered pleurisy, a rancher called Halbower whose son had suffered a wasting fever, and an Irishman named McBride who credited Kong with saving his arm from the surgeon's saw. And others, among them assorted Chinese. They were nearly unanimous in their esteem for the departed Dr. Kong. The two exceptions, Mr. Kenyon and Mr. Sweet, felt Kong's cures to be ineffective, but they had neither incurred debts nor suffered debilitations sufficient, in my opinion, to engender murderous passions.

For all my efforts, I did not uncover even one definite suspect. At last I made a foray into the camp of Mr. J. T. Smith, but the whole of my interview consisted of my greeting him at the door of his cabin and receiving, at gunpoint, his invitation to "Clear out."

It was at this juncture that the Chinaman who had brought the cat came to me again with a small bundle of papers. These had been found among Kong's possessions, and since I had taken an interest in Dr. Kong's affairs, perhaps I would know what to do about these.

The papers were promissory notes and demand drafts against accounts in the Baker City Bank. Some were years old. I thought at first that Kong may not have understood how to present the drafts at the bank, but, no, the bank employees knew him. They affirmed that they had settled paper demands on his behalf.

William, I pursued my investigation along this new line and found no suspects, but proof instead of something else. Who had written these demands that were never presented? Mrs. Wilbur, who was widowed. Mr. Addams, whose only daughter had the polio. Others, whose travails I knew from my pastoral work. Their accounts in Kong's ledger showed them owing him nothing. He'd kept the demands and notes, but I do not think he ever meant to collect them. I advised burning them.

I knew Kong better than ever, but I did not know his killer.

In memory, I revisited some of the pleasant hours I had spent with Kong. With Cloud Stalking Mice watching me from his place near the stove, I thought of how the cat had seemed a very mountain lion to those three deer. That is when I conceived a motive for the murder.

VII.

I laid my reasoning before the sheriff, but he gave it a skeptical audience. "Well then," I said, "what if we were to test the matter and see whether or not there is some truth to my supposings?" He replied that he should like to know what test I proposed.

So it was that I found myself again approaching the cabin of the well-armed Mr. Smith. I wheezed a grateful prayer as I spied him at his wood pile, ax in hand and no guns in sight. Providence might not after all require that I be shot in order to prove my conjecture, though the ax gave me a moment of disquiet. He swung it with considerable vigor for a man his age.

"Brother Smith," I hailed him when I caught my breath, "I must have a word with you."

He looked up from his labors, startled by my voice. Then he squinted. "I got nothing to say to nobody," he said. "You clear out of here."

I approached, but not too close. "You must hear me," I said. "I am worried for your sake."

"You're what?" He leaned on his ax handle to consider me.

"The man who killed that Chinaman, Kong, is in mortal danger," I said. "Justice is at hand. I fear for that man. I pray that he will make his peace with God and ask forgiveness, lest he meet his maker unrepentant."

"What's that got to do with me?" Smith asked, but I did not give any plain answer. Instead I kept at my appeal for his salvation and asked if he would not clear his soul. Was there anything he wanted to tell me by way of confession? Would he prepare his soul for judgment?

"Just what are you going on about?" Smith said.

I said, "Certain facts, once discovered, must in time be laid before the sheriff."

"What facts?" He stood straight now and hefted the ax.

Of course I did not know. I had not myself discovered whatever it was that Kong had found out, either by hearing Smith's ravings when he was delirious with fever, or perhaps by finding some clue within Smith's cabin.

"Does it matter what facts condemn a man?" I said. "I would have you know the fact by which your soul may be saved! I would have you enlist yourself with Christ before it is too late!"

Smith's face had reddened. "Damn you, what facts? What have you told the sheriff?"

"I've given him no proof of anything," I answered honestly, "for a man's soul is my first concern."

"So you think you know something what will hang me?"

"I know you must ask God for mercy."

"But you ain't told. You ain't told nobody."

"Will you accept your redeemer? Will you get down on your knees with me to pray?"

"You're a damn fool," Smith said. He advanced with his ax and made ready to swing at my head.

A gunshot rang out. Smith stopped short of my assassination and looked to where the sheriff had emerged from his cover.

What evidence had we of Smith's culpability in the Chinaman's death? None. The sheriff had not heard all of the words that passed between me and Smith. All he had seen was the murderous rage that I had predicted, and that was enough to convince him that Smith's possessions should be searched, as I had urged.

What is it but consciousness of his own sin that possesses a criminal to save a record of his misdeeds, even when that record has nearly trapped him before? Such a man is ripe for conversion, whether he knows it or not.

Among Smith's possessions were papers related to the discharge from the Union Army of one J. T. Canfield. So was his real name discovered. Along with these papers was a clipping from the Walla Walla *Statesman* which detailed the deathbed statement of Robert McMillan. He had been one of the gunmen in the Snake River massacre of twenty-one Chinese miners, and he named his companions in the crime. These were Bruce Evans, Mat LaRue, Frank Vaughn, Hiram Maynard, Carl Hughes, and J. T. Canfield. Also among Canfield's belongings was an ivory knife that was obviously of oriental manufacture. Likewise an enameled mirror.

Now you will perhaps think that I had found Canfield out by an unlikely entrapment, and you would be right except for one thing: I was but inviting him to repeat himself.

The deer had known Kong's cat to be harmless until at some moment they sensed a change in him. By his alteration, by his attempt to conceal his interest in the deer, he had instead excited their anxiety.

While treating Canfield, Kong must have made some discovery that made him suspicious. And Canfield, sensing a change, began to fear Kong. And killed him. As he would have killed me.

VIII.

I made pastoral visits to Mr. Canfield in the Baker City jail. I urged him to confess and repent. He said to me, "You know what happened up in Enterprise, preacher? They caught three of the men that was supposedly with me on the Snake River. They stood them up on trial. And the jury acquitted every last one."

Then he said, "If I kilt anyone, and I ain't saying I did, the ones kilt was Chinamen."

I feared it might be true that no jury would convict a white man. I feared also that Canfield would not repent his sins and accept heaven's embrace.

IX.

I have told you, William, that I have of late been in dark despair. But it is not for the lack of earthly justice. James Thomas Canfield was found guilty of the murder of Kong-Cheong and was sentenced soon after to hang. Canfield might have been right that a white jury would not convict a white man for the death of Chinese miners. But a jury of white patients, or the kin of patients, might convict a white man for the death of their Chinese doctor, even on the weight of circumstantial evidence.

You will think, then, that my despair may come for the loss of Canfield's soul. But Canfield was not lost. After his conviction, I continued to visit him in his cell. I urged him, as his fatal appointment neared, to be conscious of the hand that God reached down to him. I preached the terrors of judgment to him as I had never preached them before. Bit by bit, he achieved his Justification, grew aware of his sinful nature, and was touched by the merciful forgiveness of our Lord. He was lifted up by operation of the Holy Spirit! I knew with certainty that he knew the joys of regeneration, for his face was bathed in the light of glory, and he himself declared how the light had broken into his soul. We sang hymns together.

For him everything was changed. Everything, except that he must still meet his appointment with the noose.

In Canfield's company, I felt the force of his conversion, but away from him, I wrestled with a mystery. Why should Kong-Cheong, who had never wronged any man I heard of, suffer judgment and torment for his sins while Canfield, who was a murderer many times over, was redeemed?

I have never believed, as you have, that God might save some by their good works. Who has said His mercy is infinite has not read scripture. Matthew 18:3. Luke 13:3. *Except* ye be converted. *Except* ye repent.

Briefly, I conjectured to doubt the Holy Bible. What if God might show mercies not therein described? But if the Bible is not the fullness of revelation, what seals the Covenant?

Nothing can. Without the certainty that scripture is complete and true, there can be no ground for faith to stand upon.

The Bible cannot contain God full and entire, but it contains His word. We have our contract with Him. By that can we know him. What then, must I conclude from what my heart told me, that it was not justice if Canfield and Kong could not *both* be saved?

X.

At Canfield's request, I stood with him on the gallows. The executioner had covered Canfield's head, so that we spoke our partings through the black cloth. I soothed him with prayer and with scripture, though all the while my heart tripped and stammered. I was out of breath from mounting the scaffold steps, and no doubt my heart pounded for the fatality of the event. Also, I was thinking troubled thoughts. All mortal men had offended God, and none was deserving of salvation. Only by mercy were a few redeemed, not by justice. But who was God that He should count so little the ministrations of men to one another, and so greatly their acknowledgment of Him?

Canfield, though his face was shrouded in black cloth, radiated the light of his redemption. "I go to Him now! Praise God! Praise Jesus!" He trembled. I do think he trembled with joy.

XI.

I have taught Cloud Stalking Mice to sit upon my lap. His purr soothes me even as his strange gaze continues to agitate my soul. In these, my last days, he gives me some earthly consolation. Yet he troubles me, too. I watch him mousing. Some preay he tortures, then dispatches. Others, he lets go. But he knows nothing of them. They are just mice.

I have long since exhausted my supply of medicinal herbs. In Kong's absence there is no one who knows how to re-supply me. I have even abandoned the "chee gong" exercises.

William, I have taken a backward step from the ladder of Sanctification you and I first mounted together in younger days. I do not think to be perfected in love. To the ledger of my sins we may add my thoughts of late, but even those will be washed away in forgiveness. I do not despair of my salvation, but of what salvation must be.

By many names is He known. One might be Cloud Stalking Men. I may look upon Him and know ere you read this.

I wish I could rejoice in that.

In His Name,

John J. Tiller

Gravity

I have a good head for remembering things. Objects attract one another in proportion to the product of their masses and in inverse proportion to the square of their distance, that's how the equation goes. My mother had just walked out on my father. He should have seen it coming. In fact, he probably did, but he didn't say the things that could have stopped her. My father was never any good at saying the things that needed to be said.

My wife said I should go see him. I should take him something. I should get him to talk. So after work I drove over to my parents' house — my father's house, now — with the casserole Susan had baked. On the way, I stopped at a liquor store for a fifth of scotch.

Dad came to the door when I rang, and I followed him into his den, where he had been watching a baseball game. There were smudged empty glasses all around his over-stuffed chair. When he sat down again, he sank down deep into the upholstery.

"Who's pitching?" I said, and Dad said, "Stieb."

"Brought you something," I told him, and I held out the bottle. He thanked me and opened it. He poured a little scotch into one of the glasses.

"None for me," I said when he tipped the bottle toward a second glass. "Susan made you a casserole. I'll go put it in the kitchen."

Dad nodded, looking at the game. In the kitchen, I cleared away some crusty dishes and put the casserole on the counter next to a half-full glass of flat beer. Gasses are soluble in liquids in inverse proportion to temperature. Warm beer goes flat fast.

Back in the den, I watched the game with my father for a while, and then I said, "You want to talk about this?"

He looked at me, and then he looked back at the game.

I said, "I didn't think so."

Wind over Heaven

‡

Susan made me go back a few days later, with another casserole. When Dad came to the door, I noticed that his flesh sagged from his eyes and cheeks, so he looked a little like a basset hound. He was skinny as ever, but as he led the way back to his den, the floorboards groaned and popped under his footsteps. I outweighed him by a good twenty pounds, but the floor was silent under my feet. When he sat in his easy chair, Dad sank down so far into the cushion that it looked like the chair was folding in on him.

"Brought you another," I said, offering a bottle.

"Thanks."

"I'll just go put this in the kitchen," I told him, meaning the casserole. He nodded as he picked up the remote and flipped through the channels.

I found the first casserole dish where I had left it, untouched. I discovered a thin layer of mold when I lifted the lid. It was green. Molds are saprophytes. No chlorophyll. The green comes from the spores growing on the filament ends. I don't make any special effort to remember these things. Like I say, I just have a head for it. I scraped the moldy food into the garbage and joined Dad in the den.

"You should eat something," I told him.

"Yeah," he said. "I suppose." There was a motorcycle race on ESPN.

"You can't keep going on just scotch," I said. "Empty calories."

"Yeah."

A rider lost control of his bike and flipped into a hay bale. My father took a sip of his scotch.

"Did you try to talk to Mom before she left?"

When he didn't say anything, I said, "Do you know where she went?"

He shook his head and poured some scotch from his new bottle.

"Maybe she'll call," I said. "You could talk to her then."

"I'm fine," he told me. "I'm trying to watch the TV here, okay?"

I got up to go, and he struggled to rise from his chair. The floorboards creaked loudly again. One of the chair's arms made a popping sound as he tried to lever himself up against it.

"It's okay," I told him. "I know the way out."

When Dad stopped trying to get up, he fell back into the center of the chair even deeper than before. The chair legs bent outward, near collapse. I said good-bye.

"How'd it go?" Susan asked me later, and I said, "Okay."

‡

The last time I went to the house, he didn't come to the door. I let myself in, and when I checked his den, the TV was on, and I could tell that the chair had finally caved in. The splintered legs were still there, at the edge of a big square hole in the floor.

I looked down the hole, but I couldn't see anything except some uphostery threads that had caught on the shattered floor joists. I walked into the basement, and the square hole continued from there as a deep shaft through the concrete. It was so deep, in fact, that I couldn't see the bottom even when I got a flashlight from his workroom.

"Dad?" I called.

My voice echoed down the hole, unanswered.

‡

"So what happened?" Susan asked me later that night, when I brought back the casserole dishes.

"He doesn't want to talk about it," I said.

"But he's got to talk about it," Susan said. "He can't keep it all locked up inside, or there's no telling what will happen. What did you say? Did you try to draw him out?"

"I don't want to talk about it," I said.

I sat in my recliner and turned on the tube.

On Top

I was in heavy labor, about to give birth. The crew of my starship sealed me up inside the escape pod's duplicator and turned the duper on. The next thing I knew, the duper was open and I was blinking at sunshine. Natural sunshine, not the ship's artificial light. Someone was standing in the doorway of the pod, and behind her, instead of my ship, was the cracked sunlit surface of a planet. I couldn't see her clearly, silhouetted like she was. She came into the pod and took me by the arm.

"We're going to take good care of you," she said. Her voice sounded familiar.

I was a little dazed. You're always dazed coming out of a duper. I blinked as she brought me out into the sunshine, where I came face to face with a woman wearing a ragged, threadbare dress that fit her like a tent. "Get her on the table," she told the other one. I thought, *Who is this bitch and why is she wearing such a rag?* I looked at the woman who was holding my arm. She was dressed in animal skins. She had my face. Another contraction hit me, and I said "Oh shit" not just because of the pain but because it all came together for me then. These women, the one wearing animal skins and the one wearing the raggedy dress, they were both me, only older. The ragged dress was a dirty, worn-out version of the gold lamé maternity dress I was wearing.

The "table" was a large, flat boulder. There were some other boulders scattered about, but the landscape was generally flat, except for some distant hills. And everything was barren. No plants, except for little patches of reddish moss. Not a stick of wood. The crumpled escape pod, the boulders, the hills. That was *everything*.

"Lie down," said the one in the tattered dress.

"Those bastards!" I said. The crew had marooned me somewhere. They must have put the duper on stasis, then dropped the pod on the first likely planet. Just because I was expecting a little service for my money!

"Come on," said the me in animal skins. "Be a good girl. Make this easy. Lie down."

"Make what easy!" I said. "Stop telling me what to do!"

The me in the tattered dress stepped close enough for me to see the tiny wrinkles around her eyes. She pricked my neck with something. It must have been a dermal. I felt warm. My knees buckled, and the two of them laid me on their "table." The sky darkened, went black.

I heard one say to the other, "She figured it out a lot faster than you did."

"Yeah. Well, I have at least figured out *this*."

"Ouch! You bitch!"

"Oh, shut up. It's about time I had something nice."

Then I was out.

‡

Things had not gone exactly as planned during my trip among the stars, but I'm no fool. I hadn't expected things to go exactly as planned. When there were problems, I turned them into opportunities.

My oxygen concentrator was not working when I prepared to land on Penthos, the first planet on my itinerary. Did I pack up and go home? No. I had the crew set me down in the lowlands of the equatorial continent. Even there, below sea level, the atmospheric pressure was lower than it is on the summit of earth's Mount Everest. Without the concentrator, I was in agony as I breathed the thin Penthian air, but I didn't have to stay for long. And now I could say that I'd not only been to Penthos, but I had breathed that planet's natural atmosphere, unaugmented. I continued to leave breathing gear — filters, reducers, concentrators, deodorizers — on the ship wherever we set down, making my accomplishment all the more impressive.

Then there was my pregnancy. From the moment I hired him, I had planned to seduce my captain, a gorgeous young man named Connell N. Dunnich who wasn't *anybody* yet, though I thought that with his looks and his youth he was bound to go places in his career. Rumors of a liaison between us would be newsworthy. I'd get him into the news feeds and gossip squirts. Later, when he was famous in his own right, stories about him would still carry a link to me. Leveraged publicity, I call it, where each enhances the other's profile.

But having his baby? Having a baby at all? Not in my plans. Not in my plans *at all*.

But I didn't end the pregnancy, not when I'd considered the opportunity it presented. After my adventure was over, people at the cocktail parties would say, "That's Maura Voss. Not only was she the first person to visit all eighty-eight home worlds of the Stellar Civilizations (breathing their natural air, no less), but she did it while she was *pregnant*!"

Also, people have always done what I've told them to do because I'd pay them money. But a child does what you tell it because it *has* to. Mommy's the boss. I liked that, too.

Finally, there was the biggest problem of all. After I'd set foot on eighty-four of the eighty-eight home worlds, I had to contend with the war between the Deeble Moons and Maconis. By the time my ship arrived in their arm of the galaxy, these two worlds had thrown enough blast energy and hard radiation at each other to wreck both of their economies. There could be no winner, but Deeble and Maconis fought on anyway. Space around their suns was full of killer robots, and atomic warheads dodged their way across the void and into the home world atmospheres.

Problem? No. Opportunity!

If I managed to set foot on both places before they had obliterated one another, then I could not only be the first woman to have visited the eighty-eight Stellar Civilizations. I would have a chance to be the *only* person to have visited all eighty-eight worlds while there were still eighty-eight to visit.

Unfortunately, my crew argued with me. They refused to see the opportunity for what it was. They complained about the risks. I was paying them well, they admitted, but not enough for a suicide mission.

These people had come with references. They were supposed to be loyal. They were supposed to deliver me where I wanted to go. After Captain Conn parked the ship in a remote orbit around the Deeble sun, I tried to remind them all of that in a meeting on the bridge. Since they would all be wearing the green and blue uniforms I had designed myself — I've always had a flair for fashion — I showed up wearing mine. As a reminder. Mine had even more gold braid on the shoulders than Conn's uniform.

Counting the doctor, three of the crew members were women, but my uniform was also the only one with a slit skirt. I have nice legs, and I don't mind who knows it. They still looked good, even though the rest of my figure was temporarily shot. Use everything you've got in a crisis.

"We can still go to the next two worlds on your list," Conn said a the meeting. "Willaan. Gilm. You'll have visited all eighty-six planets that *surviving* Stellar Civilizations."

"And then somebody else can come along," I said, "and visit those same eighty-six easy-to-visit worlds. Worse, someone who has already visited Deeble and Maconis could visit the eighty-six others and trump my record! No. Not acceptable."

"Maura," said the ship's doctor, whose name isn't worth remembering, "Why is this so important to you?"

She had been with me all this time, and she didn't get it? I could have told her about being rich. How it's no distinction at all. Or being beautiful. How so many millions of rich, beautiful women live on all the crowded worlds and across the far reaches of space. How money and beauty are nothing. What matters is having done something. That's what makes you special. That's what puts you on top.

Instead, I told her, "Don't call me Maura. You have a contractual obligation to me, which you all seem to have forgotten. Call me Ms. Voss."

Conn said, "Now, Maura . . ."

"Ms. Voss," I insisted. "You think you're special just because you've got a bun in the boss's oven?" I patted my swollen belly through my uniform.

He paled.

I looked at all of them, at Conn, the doctor, and the other seven members of the crew. Except for Conn, none of them had a name worth remembering now. I said, "Review your contracts, people. If you don't take me to Deeble and Maconis, it's going to cost you. Penalties. Fines. I get what I want. The contracts are written to make sure of that. One negative report, one data squirt from me to my trust fund, and you're all down to base union scale for this whole trip."

"Union scale?" someone said. I knew that more than one of them was planning to retire on the proceeds from this trip. But they couldn't do that with four years of pay at union scale.

"Ms. Voss," said Conn slowly. His face was red now. "Reconsider. This crew has bent over backwards for you until now. They've endured . . ." He pursed his lips. "They have acquiesced to every reasonable request and not a few that weren't so reasonable. That picnic on the rim of the volcano. The photos of your EVA jaunt in the Brecose asteroids. But this is no warship. We can't evade killer bots. We don't have shields against blast forces or hard rads."

"You're smart, hon," I said. "I hired you for your brains, even if the rest of you isn't bad at all. So use those brains. Figure out a way through their defenses. I want what I want. And I do get what I want. And don't you ask me again to reconsider, because you all know I'm not going to change my mind."

Then I left them all on the bridge to think it over. In my quarters, I stripped off my uniform and programmed wardrobe duper for a party dress in gold lamé. I was sure they'd come around. I really do get what I want. And when they called me on the comm to say that they would be good boys and girls after all, I wanted clothes that said *money* and *charm*, rather than *I'm the boss*. I had to try on three versions of the dress, recycling the ones that weren't quite right and reprogramming the duper, before I found one that sent the right message and still worked as a maternity dress.

But hours later, they still hadn't called to apologize, and I went into labor. Things got . . . complicated. I called the doctor on the comm. When she showed up, there were two other crew members with her. To help me to the duper, they said.

"The duper?" I said. "I don't need to be backed up! I need a pain killer! This is *very* uncomfortable!"

"Birth is a tricky business," the physician said. "Always will be." She looked at the two crewmen, and they stared hard at her. Her look and theirs might have said a lot to me if I'd been paying close attention. But my mind was on the sensation of little vices pinching me from the inside. "We need you copied in case anything goes wrong," the doctor said. "For the baby's sake."

"Fine!" I said. "But give me something for the pain!"

She ignored that. The crewmen stood on either side of me, as if I might fall over. As if they needed to guard me.

"This way," one of them said.

"But the duper is . . ."

"Being serviced. We need to use the one in the escape pod."

I should have thought right then, *The escape pod? They have to dupe me in the escape pod?* But I could think only about how another contraction would keep coming soon, and the doctor really should give me something to disconnect me from it.

The whole crew met us at the pod. Conn was there. As they opened the pod and strapped me into the duper, Conn said, "Are you sure you won't reconsider, Maura? About Deeble and Maconis?"

And still I didn't suspect a thing. I said, "If you'd worked something out instead of parking us way out here, I could be having this baby on Deeble. During a war. Think of the press *that* would have gotten!"

Wind over Heaven

‡

The dermal didn't keep me unconscious for long. It was another contraction that brought me around. A bad one. And I woke to find that my wrists and ankles were tied to the stone table with leather strips. I was naked. When I turned my head, I saw that the me who wore the tattered version of the lamé dress was lying gagged and hog-tied on the ground, glaring at the other version of me, the one that had worn animal skins. Now she was wearing my dress.

"Now it's *your* turn to be the new one," said the me in the new dress.

"What is this?" I said. "Are you crazy?"

"My words, exactly, when it happened to me," she said.

A dirty little boy in a leather loin cloth came skipping across the dusty ground. He stopped and stared at me.

"Go do something," said the me in the new dress.

"What?" said the boy. He had the eyes of Captain Conn Dunnich.

"I don't know. Go play with Dunnich."

"He doesn't want to play with me."

"Well just go!"

But the kid didn't go. He backed off a little, then hung around, watching me give birth.

‡

After the me in the lamé dress had untied my right hand and my right foot so I could lie on my side and nurse the baby, a second boy showed up. He, too, wore skins and had the captain's eyes, as he naturally would. He had acne. This boy looked on sullenly as the me in my dress covered me up with an animal skin.

"Can't have the boys ogling you," she said. "It embarrasses me."

"I want my dress back," I said.

"It's not yours anymore." She untied the other me, the one wearing the tattered copy of the dress. Once the older me had spit out her gag, she said, "That dress is *mine*!"

"It's my turn," said the other one.

"Who says you get a turn? I've been here the longest! I can't believe how ungrateful you are!"

"I should be grateful? For what? For getting to wait on you like some servant?"

They went on bickering about which of them should have my dress as if the thought would never occur to them that maybe I wanted it, too, and since I'd brought it with me, it was *mine*.

All my life, I have been surrounded by selfish people. I can't stand selfishness. I really can't.

"Somebody come take this baby away," I said. "I need some rest. And untie me!"

A deep voice said, "I see she has arrived."

I looked up and saw him, a grown man casually gripping a rifle with one hand. In the other, he held a furry little corpse. "Conn?" I said. "You're here too?"

"He is," said me in the lamé dress. "But he's not the Conn you're thinking of."

I saw what she meant. This wasn't the captain, who had been my lover. This was my son, the baby who dozed at my breast, but grown.

"Conn," said the other me, "tell Three that the dress is mine. I've been counting on it!"

"Two is the boss," Conn said. "That's the rule. Oldest has seniority."

And the boy with acne said, "That sucks!"

"Yeah," said the me who wore my dress. "It stinks!"

"Could be worse," Conn said. "You could still be the newest." He pointed at me. "You could be *her*."

I decided that I didn't like him. I did not like him at all.

‡

I was Four. That's what they called me. And they didn't untie me until they explained how things worked.

The escape pod's big duper had been reprogrammed. It didn't contain molecular maps for the whole crew of my ship any longer. It was a lifeboat for just me and my unborn baby. And it had been damaged in the crash landing on the planet's surface so that it took a long time to assemble mass from the air and process duplications. It made one of me once every eight standard years.

The pod's food duper produced only emergency rations and water condensed from the atmosphere. So the survival gear was limited to the items that had already been on the ship, including a duper rifle that could make its own bullets from air and sunlight, an EVA suit, and assorted tools. The signaling gear had all been removed. We weren't ever going home.

The first of me to arrive, One, had taken charge of the rifle and used it to keep Two in line. Later, One let Conn take charge of the rifle and enforce the seniority rule.

So Two was One's slave, until One disappeared. And then Three was a slave for Two. Now I was supposed to be a slave for both of them. The baby was my responsibility, but as soon as I could, I was supposed to do whatever else they wanted me to do, too.

The oldest boy was Conn. The teenager was Dunnich. The

youngest, until I arrived, was Enn. Two, once she had made Three take off my dress and hand it over, said I couldn't name the baby after his father. Conn, Enn, and Dunnich were all taken. It was a rule.

"I'll call him whatever I want to," I told the bitch. "He's my baby."

"Don't be selfish," she said. "All the captain's names are already taken."

"He didn't speak up and keep the crew from marooning me here," I said. "I don't *want* to name my baby for him."

"Good. Because you *can't*."

I don't like being told that I can't do things. So I said, "His name is Captain."

"That's stupid," said Three.

"That's what I'm naming him."

"It's not a name!"

"It is now."

"You can't!"

But Conn spoke up. He said, "It's her right."

"But . . ."

"Just shut up," said Conn. He looked at me. "Her baby. She decides. Now somebody untie her and give her something to wear."

"That would be *your* job," Two said to Three.

I felt like hell, but I gave Conn a nice smile. A nice smile for that twenty-four-year-old copy of my baby. He blushed and stalked away, taking his rifle with him.

I thought I might like him after all.

‡

Day after day, I nursed the baby. And after a while, I had other jobs. Three showed me how to scrape the hides from the little animals that Conn hunted in the hills, how to stretch the hides on the hull of the escape pod and tan them. We couldn't eat the animals. Their flesh was alien, indigestible. But the skins were useful, especially as diapers. Two said life had been a lot harder when she'd first come, and there *weren't* any animals. Without enough water for laundering, so I scraped and tanned a lot of skins, and I half wished there weren't any animals now, either.

There wasn't any cooking to do, but I served the rations as the little duper extruded them. I cleaned the plates.

I knew I couldn't live this way for long. I just knew it. Three had probably felt the same way, and Two before her, but I knew that I absolutely had to find a way to come out on top, to be the important person I knew I really was. Somehow. Things would be different for me. I wasn't just *anybody*, after all.

For a long time, I stewed every day as I watched Two and Three, watched the boys, cared for Captain. I thought about things.

Whenever the boys or I did something Two or Three didn't like, there would be a new rule, and Conn would enforce it. Sometimes, Two overruled rules that Three made.

Conn didn't make any rules, but he was subject to them. Two reminded him that he wasn't to go into the forest. The forest somewhere beyond the hills was the source of the animals he hunted, but he was only allowed to take the ones that had wandered outside of it. "If you go into that forest again," Two would say, "I just *know* you will lose the rifle. And we need the rifle."

"I won't," Conn would say. "It's a rule."

"Well, remember that."

She didn't need to tell him that. Conn seemed utterly convinced of the correctness and the necessity of Two's rules.

Time passed, though you couldn't tell. Every day was about the same as the day before. The baby grew, but it would be a while before it was old enough that it would have to obey me. The chronometer on the duper advanced, showing how long it would be before the duper made another Maura. Maura Five. But it would take even longer for her to be made than it would take for Captain to be obedient. Eight years less a few weeks is still almost eight years. I wasn't going to wait that long if I could help it.

At last, I figured things out. I decided that it was necessary to like Conn. And to have him like me back. A lot.

He had the rifle. He enforced the rules. If he wanted to, someday he could *change* the rules. And more than once I caught him looking at me in a way that is not the way a son looks at his mother.

So while I pretended not to notice his longing looks, I sewed a new dress of skins. Three took that from me, so I sewed another one that was just as good. I stayed out of the sun for the sake of my skin. I washed.

The more I thought about Conn, the more I realized that he was the one thing really worth having. With or without his rifle, he was a prize.

One morning when Conn left early to go hunting in the hills while Two and Three were sleeping, I followed him into the hills. When I caught up, he asked me what I wanted.

I told him.

"But you're my mother," he said, blushing, but looking directly into my eyes. "Two said it would be wrong when Three wanted to."

"Three wanted to?" That bitch. She had hatched the same plan before I'd come.

"Yes, but Two said . . ."

"Three is too old for you," I said. "That's what was wrong. The age difference. Believe me, Conn. It's all right. We're the same age, so it's all right." I stepped close to him. "It's wrong for you to grow up and not know about women."

"Two said I shouldn't."

"With Three." I kissed him, and my hands reached inside of his leather clothes. "You shouldn't do it with Three."

He didn't tell be to stop, but he said weakly, "It's a rule."

"There can't be any rule that you're never allowed to be with a woman. And who else is there but me?"

My hands found what they were looking for. He shuddered.

"Besides," I said, "aren't you old enough to make up your own mind about things? Aren't you old enough to make some of your own rules?"

"No, I'm not," he whispered. "Two says . . ." Then, as I did the next thing that I did, he groaned.

‡

He wasn't as good as his father. But then, he hadn't had any practice, either. In any case, what mattered was that *he* have a good time. What mattered was that he'd want more of the same later, and would want to stay on my good side.

We were lying in the shade of a boulder. He said, "Aren't you worried about the baby?"

"Two will take care of him. Or Three."

"But you're the one who's supposed to. You're the newest. It's your job. That's the rule!"

"Conn, did you ever stop to think that the rules might be stupid?"

He looked puzzled. "The rules are the *rules*," he said at last, as if that settled everything for him. "I don't break the rules. Nobody can break the rules."

"You can, Conn. You've got the rifle. You can make new rules!" I caressed his face. "Didn't you like what we just did together, Conn? Wouldn't you like to do it again tomorrow and the next day?"

"Yes," he said. "But that doesn't mean . . ."

"Conn, I want you to take charge. Two doesn't make good rules. Together, you and I will make much better rules."

"But Two's rules are stronger than anyone's. She'd just say our rules were wrong."

"And why do we have to listen to what she says!"

He pondered this. "It's a rule?"

Bruce Holland Rogers

"Conn," I said, "sometimes it's all right to break a rule. Sometimes breaking a rule is the best thing you can do."

"Not for me."

"Are you kidding?" I said. "You just broke about the biggest rule there is! It's a bigger rule than anything Two ever made. You just had sex with your mother!"

"*One* was my mother," Conn said, blushing. "You're Four."

"I'm exactly the same as her, Conn, and you know it. I'm your mother! Back where we all come from, having sex with your mother is very, very wrong! It's a huge, important rule! But didn't you *like* it, Conn? Didn't you enjoy breaking that rule?"

"You tricked me! You said it was okay!"

"For us, yes," I said. "We have to make our own rules!"

He stood up and adjusted his leather clothes.

"Conn," I said, standing beside him. "It's all right. Nothing bad happened, see? We just broke a rule, and everything is fine! Better than before!"

"What if I broke other rules?" he said. "What if I went into the forest? We might lose the rifle forever!"

"That's stupid, Conn! Why would you lose the rifle?"

"Because the forest won't let me bring it in!" he said. "Two can't go into the forest. And Three can't. The forest won't let them in. It would let me in, I think, but it won't let me bring the gun. It's the rule. The forest's rule."

"Conn," I said, "what are you talking about? Forests don't make rules."

"Oh, they don't? Then you just try to enter the forest. You're a Maura. The forest won't let you in!"

"I don't believe you," I said, not sure whether I believed him or not. "Show me."

He hesitated. "You're supposed to take care of the baby." Then he turned around and walked away, headed further into the hills. That wasn't exactly an invitation to follow him, but I followed anyway.

‡

The furry little animals that Conn hunted never appeared close to the escape pod, and they were rare even in the nearby hills. But as Conn walked toward the highest ridges and then down the other side, I saw more and more dark shapes scurrying among the boulders. And in the valley below, I saw the forest.

It wasn't anything like any forests I'd seen before on all the many worlds I had been to. Those were always vast, irregular landscapes of trees. This forest was perfectly round. The edge of the forest, all the way around, was black. Then, beyond that ring of black growth were trees as tall and green as any I had ever seen.

"It's . . . different," I said. But Conn didn't hear me. He was still far ahead of me, striding determinedly and never even glancing back to see if I was following.

When he got to the edge of the forest, he still didn't look back, but he stood still as if waiting for me. Or maybe he was just thinking things over.

Up close, the forest perimeter looked even less like anything I had seen anywhere else. The undergrowth of black, fleshy bushes had neither leaves nor thorns, but something more like both together. Above these rose . . . I can't quite call them trees. They were leafless, articulated like skeletal black arms and claws. Vines and ragged webs twined among these forbidding plants. And they moved. Black tendrils snaked slowly toward Conn.

I said, "Conn! Look out!"

"It's all right. The forest likes me." Sure enough, the tendrils palpated him, perhaps tasted him, and drew back. The black bushes parted as if to invite him into the forest. "It won't like you," he said. "It doesn't like Mauras."

I took that as a challenge. I stepped toward the opening that the forest had made for Conn. As the black tendrils reached me, though, and as they tasted me, they twined around my ankles. The passage that had opened for Conn now closed, and the bony vegetative hands bent forward toward me, fingers clasping and unclasping like hungry jaws yawning open and snapping shut.

"They won't hurt you," Conn said. "But they'll stop you."

I managed to tug my feet free and take a step forward, but the forest closed in before me, dense and impassable. When I took another step anyway, and another, the black bushes pricked and scraped my skin and the skeletal trees closed their fingers around me.

"See?" Then Conn stepped forward. While still barring my way, the forest parted for him a second time. "The forest has rules that we can't break!" As he spoke, black tendrils twined over him, not impeding Conn, but searching. When they came to the gun, they wrapped themselves around it. "I can enter the forest," he said. "I just can't bring the gun with me."

"All right," I admitted, backing away from the prickles. "So the forest does have some rules. But the forest is *here*. Most of the time, we're over *there*." I pointed over the hills, back toward where the escape pod was. "We can still make our own rules away from the forest."

Bruce Holland Rogers

But Conn wasn't listening to me. He was gazing into the forest, into the place that invited him, but where he wasn't allowed to go. Wasn't allowed by Two, anyway. Two's rule and the forest's rules seemed to be at odds. "It wasn't always here," Conn said. "One used to walk around a lot, looking for a place that was different. Sometimes she took me along. And there wasn't any forest here. No animals. Not until after One was gone."

"You think she's in there."

He didn't answer. He just kept looking into the forest. Finally, he said, "She must know I need the rifle. She doesn't want to take it away from me. I'm just not supposed to bring it into the forest." He let go of the stock and barrel. The vines held on to the gun, keeping it poised a meter above the ground. "I can come back for it."

I wasn't sure what I wanted him to do. I wasn't sure what would be to my best advantage, but I had my eyes on the rifle as Conn stepped forward into the opening that the forest made. Over his shoulder, he said, "Go back to the baby." Then the forest closed behind him. As it did, the rifle dropped to the ground.

One thing about the forest: It was slow to react. The vines had to detect me and decide that I was Maura before the forest could bar my way. Being slow didn't matter when it came to keeping me out of the forest. If I were to run ten meters into the forest before the tendrils knew I was there, there were still another twenty meters of bushes and bony trees to stop me. But the forest's slow reaction did make a difference if my goal was short of getting all the way into the forest.

I backed away, waited a while, and then darted forward to where the rifle lay. I snatched the gun off the ground and backed away even as the forest closed in before me. Then I sat down on the ground. I inspected the gun. To make sure that I knew how it worked, I shot a finger from one of the trees. The report didn't sound like much — just a flat *pop*, but the tree's finger exploded at the joint.

I waited for Conn. Even though I had the gun and had no plans of relinquishing it to him, I still wanted Conn. Next to the gun, Conn was the one thing most worth possessing.

I waited a long time, until I heard a dismayed howl from deep in the forest. I couldn't be sure, but I thought it was Conn's voice. None of the animals he hunted had ever made a sound.

The howl was the kind of sound that told me Conn wasn't coming out. At least not on his own. If I wanted him, I was probably going to have to go in and get him. So I thought about how I might do that. I thought about how the forest seemed to know by smell who was Conn and who was a Maura. I hatched a plan.

I do get what I want.

‡

I didn't see Dunnich anywhere near the escape pod. He was probably off sulking somewhere. Enn was standing next to a pile of little stones he'd made, and he was throwing them, one at a time, at some larger stones. Two was sitting in the shade next to the pod. When she saw me coming, the first thing she said was, "Where have *you* been." Then she saw the gun. "Where's Conn?"

"In the forest," I said.

Three came out of the escape pod. She was holding Captain. She looked furious. "If you think we did your chores for you —" she started to say. Then she, too, noticed the gun.

"Give that to me," Two said, getting up and coming toward me.

I leveled the rifle at her.

She hesitated, but kept coming. "You wouldn't," she said.

I smiled. "Would you?"

She froze.

"Yeah, I thought so. Now both of you get away from the pod." When they had backed off sufficiently, I went into the pod and gabbed the EVA suit. I warned them to stay put.

It took me a long time to drag the suit halfway into the hills. I stopped to make sure they hadn't followed me, then I put the suit on. It was hot inside, until I got the life support switched on. I set the comm gear for two-way external, so I could hear and be heard. Then I resumed my walk toward the forest.

I had figured it this way: The forest wanted Conn to come to it. It didn't want him to bring his rifle — afraid of what he might do with it maybe. But it did want Conn, and it knew how to tell Conn apart from Two or Three or me.

One, I guessed, was behind that forest. She wanted her baby back.

It must have been very different for her, landing here alone.

When I got to the forest, I moved very slowly towards the perimeter. Even though the EVA suit wouldn't smell or taste like a human being, I thought the plants might sense motion. Sure enough, the tendrils did snake out toward me. I froze as one of them wrapped around my ankle, tip probing the surface of the suit. Then the tendril dropped away and withdrew.

Other tendrils brushed over the EVA suit as I passed, but desultorily, as if they weren't convinced that I was there at all. I kept moving the rifle out of their reach, afraid that they might recognize

Bruce Holland Rogers

its scent. Step by step, slowly, I made my way past the perimeter and into the forest proper.

The trees soared skyward. The ground between them was carpeted with moss and white flowers. Through the suit's comm, I heard the buzz of insects, and in the shadows of the trees I saw little furry animals grazing on the moss.

I didn't see any sign of Conn, so I pressed on, going deeper into the forest. The trees grew taller and thicker, the shadows deeper. I stumbled over a fleshy protuberance growing up from the ground and sprawled onto a patch of these growths. They were egg-shaped, but covered with throbbing veins. One of them peeled open, and I watched an animal slick with the fluid of its birth tumble out. As I stood, I noticed that the tree trunks were studded with smaller, crustier growths. An insect struggled to emerge from one.

I pressed on, until at last I came to a clearing. At the far edge of the clearing rustled a great, leafy green mass. Only when it stood up could I see that it wasn't just a rounded hump of brush. Ten meters tall, it had two legs. Its arms and hands were covered in what looked like tree bark, except that it was supple, maybe even soft. There was a helmet-shaped bole at the top.

It had its back to me and had been tending to something near the ground. Now I could see what that something was: Conn. He was sitting on a sort of wooden throne, his arms and legs bound by living vines. His eyes were wide with terror, but purple vines filled his mouth and grew into his ears. He couldn't cry out. Perhaps he couldn't hear.

I raised the rifle and said, "Let him go."

I had already guessed that the long-absent One had been behind the forest somehow. Still, I wasn't prepared to see my own wasted face and wasted body hanging by vines from where the vegetable giant's face would have been, had it possessed a face of its own. The vines held her, arms out, like a woman crucified.

I didn't look good. That is, One, the original me, looked pale and skeletal and sick.

I pointed my rifle at her head and said again, "Let him go."

She said, "He's mine," but she didn't say it like I would have. It didn't sound the way it would have sounded coming from Two or Three. She sounded sad, regretful. "He's mine. He's all I have."

"What about all of this?" I said, waving my hand at the forest. "This whole forest is yours, right? You control it somehow. Isn't that enough?"

She lifted her emaciated face to look this way and that. "This forest is *me*," she said. "I've been alone. All alone." She looked at

Conn. "He was all I had, for such a long time. Then another came, but she was . . . she didn't understand what it had been to be alone. And then I was lost. I was more alone than ever."

She wasn't like me at all, I realized. All that time alone, before Two had arrived, had done something to her. It had been just her and Conn for eight years, and babies aren't much company. She had lost her edge.

"You shouldn't come here," she said. "This place is just for me and him." A leafy giant hand stroked Conn's face. He was looking at me, I think, saying with his eyes what he could not say with his vine-choked mouth.

"He doesn't belong to you now," I told her. "He's not a baby. He's a man. He's *mine*."

"You can't have him." The giant body turned. "He'll be like me now."

"Which means what? What are you?"

She told me, then, about the hole. She had been ranging far from the escape pod, going as far as she could go in search of water on the planet's surface. She was sure that there must be more to this world, more hospitable regions, if only she could find sources of water along some route leading out of the desert. For years she had searched this way, going as far from the escape pod as she could before thirst would drive her back again. And one dusky evening, she smelled water. She saw a hole in the ground. She went to it, knelt down, and was certain that she did in fact smell water. Deep down in the hole. She leaned forward, reaching into the darkness she could not see, hoping to graze the surface with her fingertips. And she fell. She fell and struck stone and nearly died. Tendrils found her. Tendrils that had waited for long, long years found her, and entered her body through her ears, her mouth, her nose, her eyes.

"It was a garden waiting for the return of its gardener," she said. She turned her head so I could see the purple vines snaking from the base of her skull. "The garden taught me what it was. It taught me how to shape the life forms in the well, how to grow them out into the sunlight, how to make them whatever I wanted. I grew the forest. Everything here is mine. Is me. But I can't leave. To sustain me, to keep me alive, the garden has . . . changed me. Not even my flesh is flesh."

Her arms, the arms of her white, emaciated body, were fixed to the tree by vines that grew around them. I now saw that they grew *through* her flesh as well. She couldn't bend her arms. But she could move her wrists, her hands. She opened her palms to me. A flower sprouted from the flesh of her right hand as I watched. The flesh of her left hand swelled, split, and spilled out an enormous black beetle that tumbled to the ground.

"How sad for you," I said. "I mean it. But you have to let Conn go."

"He's mine. He was always mine, and I'm taking him back."

"You made the animals and sent them out of the forest because you thought they would bring him here eventually."

"He's a smart boy."

I looked at Conn. He was definitely looking at me, pleading with his eyes. Get him out of this, and he'd be mine forever. I'd have the gun and his absolute loyalty.

"But you wouldn't let him bring his rifle into the forest. As badly as you wanted him back, you instructed the forest not to let him bring the gun. So even transformed, you must be vulnerable." I aimed at her head. "My guess is that your brain is still the original equipment. My guess is that a head shot would kill you."

"Kill me," she said, "and he dies. Already, he isn't breathing on his own. The garden breathes for him."

Out of the corner of my eye, I saw green movement around Conn. "Stop it," I said, not daring to drop my aim. "Whatever you're doing, stop!"

The green movement ceased, but then the rifle moved of its own accord. The barrel pointed away. I tried to swing it back, and couldn't.

I looked down at my arms. Vines had grown over my shoulders. I tried to step away from them, but my legs wouldn't move. Vines had grown around them, too. Through the EVA suit, I hadn't felt them.

Now I looked at Conn. The green motion had resumed. Vines were growing up all over him, sealing him from view.

"He is my son," she said. "He is mine to keep." Then the vegetable giant that was her second body turned away from me, crouched next to the vines that shrouded Conn, and was still. More vines emerged from the forest and wove themselves around her until she and Conn had both disappeared.

I was afraid that she might leave me where I was. She didn't. The vines holding my arms and legs relaxed enough for me to step out of them. I didn't linger.

‡

In this one case, I had not managed to get everything I wanted. I did have the rifle, but I had lost Conn.

On the other hand, I had gained some information. As I said

from the beginning, I'm no fool. Things often don't go exactly as planned. But when there are problems, I turn them into opportunities.

I went back to the escape pod just long enough to make Two and Three sew me some waterskins. They didn't do a very good job. The skins leaked. So I cut the helmet off of the EVA suit and used that to carry water. It was awkward to carry, but it let me go out onto the desert, searching.

Sometimes when I'd come back for food and more water, Three would say, "What about the baby?" and Two would add, "Captain is *your* baby, Four."

And I'd hold up the rifle and say, "New rules." And they took care of Captain.

Dunnich came around now only to eat and drink. He spent a lot of time in the hills, sulking, I'm sure, because he couldn't have Conn's gun even now that Conn wasn't around to claim it. He would have made trouble eventually, given the chance.

I never let them, Dunnich, Two, or Three, get close enough to even think about taking the gun from me. I only slept when I was out on the desert, away from them.

It took many days of searching. But I found it. I found a deep well in the desert. When I peered in, I could see the tentacles down there. Way down there.

It wasn't even that far from the escape pod, which made the next part easier. Even stripped of all the parts we wouldn't need any more, the pod was heavy. Two, Three, and the two boys could only drag the pod a short distance every day while I supervised with Captain on one hip and the rifle on the other.

And when the pod was close enough to the well, I said to Two, "You can keep that dress for now," because I knew she'd been expecting me to ask for it back. But I wouldn't be needing it for a while.

The first thing I threw into the well was the rifle. One had taught me that it was dangerous, having a thing like that around.

Then I sat on the lip of the well. I peered down into the darkness beyond my dangling legs.

What if I were wrong to do this? What if Two and Three had every bit as much right to come out on top as I did? Maybe we could work something out so that we would *all* be winners in the end. Weren't they, after all, really just like me?

But they weren't me. They weren't me exactly, because I *felt* so much like me. And just the fact that I was about to come out on top was a sign that I was more myself than either of them. I get what I want. That's part of what makes me, me.

So the second thing I threw into the well was . . . myself.

As far as Two and Three were concerned, I just disappeared. After a while, a forest grew up around them. A forest like One's, only in this forest, the escape pod was inside the perimeter and the perimeter vines and bushes and bony hands weren't programmed to keep some people out. No. My perimeter kept everybody in.

I never will get to visit all eighty-eight worlds of the Stellar Civilizations. I won't get to finish on top in that particular way. But here inside the forest, I make the rules now. They all do what I say. Every eight years, we get a new Maura and a new baby.

And every eight years, I get a new dress.

The Apple Golem

Das ist die alte, alte Liebesgeschichte.

‡

Baltasar wearied of the affairs of princes. They built their fiefdoms into kingdoms and their kingdoms into empires. Then they died, and their sons brought everything to dust. New princes arose, and their wars echoed the wars of their forebears like the notes of a tune heard too often, too often. Such things happened as they had always happened, and they would go on, Baltasar knew, for a very long time, with Baltasar there to witch the weather and concoct the poisons and cast the oracles, or without him.

So, he thought, *let it be without*.

‡

He followed the path into the mountains, and went on where there was no path, between the knife-edged peaks and across the fields of ice. On the other side, in another country, he descended into forest. There was a place where apple trees grew wild and each year dropped hard and bitter fruit. Here Baltasar built a hut of stones and lived in silence.

‡

How did he live? Did he draw some vital substance from the very air? Did sunlight nourish him? Perhaps it was simpler than that. He might have set snares. Mushrooms abounded in that black soil. He might have eaten of the apples.

‡

In silence, he lived. In silence, and alone.

‡

And finally, it began to gnaw at him, the old, old hunger. It worried at his bones all winter long, nameless, keeping him from sleep as the snows piled soft and deep.

‡

Spring came. Still the hunger was with Baltasar, and still he had no name for it. Then overnight, the apple blossoms opened all at once. Baltasar, blinking in their morning whiteness, clutched at his cloak. In their perfume, he recognized and named the hunger. Once named, it gnawed at him all the harder.

‡

With summer, green apples grew heavy on the trees. Baltasar began to pick them, and with a little knife, he peeled and shaped the fruit. Artfully, he pieced the silvery flesh together on his table, joining piece to piece with wooden slivers, and by some craft he knew, he kept it from corruption. The fruit did not turn brown or shrivel in the air. Long days he worked, correcting often for some flaw that he perceived, sometimes starting over, until the feet that he had carved and pieced from apple flesh lay finished on the table.

‡

And then he made the legs, from apples growing rounder on their branches. Into the night sometimes he worked, seeing by a witch-light that he conjured in his room. The hips were broad, but not unseemly so. Delicately, he carved her apple heart and lungs, covered them in apple ribs, and overlaid her chest in apple skin. Shoulders, then. Her arms. Her hands.

‡

Her face was the labor of a week. Green-apple-skinned he made her, save for her red-skinned lips and the areolae of her breasts.

‡

"Live," he said, and other words, such as his kind would know. And then he kissed her, touching with his pulsing tongue her apple-tasting one.

‡

She blinked. She stirred. And even as he lingered in the kiss, she began to move beneath him. He touched her apple knee, the yielding, now-warm skin of her apple-flesh-made thigh. He felt along the length of her, and where he touched her skin it knit together and was whole. His fingers traced her cheeks, her lips, and gently crossed her throat. He caressed her breasts and sides, breathed softly on her eyes to make them clear. When his hands had brushed her everywhere, brought all of her to life, he pressed his knee between her legs to make her yield.

‡

The thing that gnawed at him no longer gnawed. For a time, Baltasar was satisfied. He lived as he had lived before.

Bruce Holland Rogers

‡

The apple golem, after that first night, lived among the apple trees, moving in the forest shadows like a wild thing, silent. Baltasar, searching, could never quite catch sight of her. Always, it seemed, she was in the corner of his eye, then gone. But she was obedient. She came to Baltasar whenever his need was upon him, and in silence, she did as he required. Even when the leaves fell, when the last apples came to earth, when the snows began to descend heavy and wet, she remained among the trees and was with him only when he summoned her.

‡

And when the first snows turned to ice and the later snows began to fall soft and deep, something again began to gnaw at Baltasar. He called the golem, and she came to him. He looked at her, standing warm and naked in the brittle cold of his doorway. Her skin was green and supple as spring buds. Her eyes met his plainly, frankly. She would do anything, anything at all that he commanded. *This is not enough*, he thought.

He seized her wrist. She did not resist him. He pulled her sharply against him, fell with her to the floor. He bruised her flesh with his fingers, pinched and pulled at the green skin of her breasts. He battered her with his hands, grabbed sharply at her neck to force her against him. She went willingly.

Not enough, he thought. *This is not enough.*

He coupled with her, battered her, clutched hard at the flesh of her hips. When release came to him, it was not release enough. He lay still, and she gazed into his eyes as before, malleable. His creature. Too much his creature.

He pulled her closer, roughly caressed her neck. The apple smell of her skin was strong. He pressed his tongue against her shoulder, tasting, probing. And then dug his teeth into her, bit down hard even as she began to pull away. His teeth met. She rolled away from him, and her mouth was open in a soundless cry as her fingers touched emptiness he had made in her.

Yes, Baltasar thought.

She would not meet his gaze.

‡

She would not meet him with her eyes again. She was his. She could not fail to come when he called, but that frank gaze had left her. If he took her face with his hand, her eyes would dart to the side.

Yes. This was what he had longed for.

‡

All that winter, he had her. All that winter, he was free of the thing that had gnawed at him. Nearly every day, he satisfied his appetite for her, taking small bites from her shoulders, her neck, her breasts and her legs. Nearly every day, he would call to her and always she would come, but always her eyes were elsewhere.

‡

In the spring, she was a skeleton of silvery apple flesh, darting between the trees where the apple blossoms were starting. As before, he continued to summon her nearly every day, and every day he marveled at how she had begun to change. At first, it was only the smell of her, the rich scent of apple blossoms that clung to her and aroused him as never before. But when the apple tree buds began to open, when the leaves began to uncurl, the golem's wounds began to heal. The flesh that grew into the wounds was pink. When he bit it, it did not yield so easily to his teeth, and it tasted not so much like apple flesh as meat and blood. The apple golem seemed all the more pained, all the more frightened, when he bit these places. To Baltasar's delight.

‡

It could entertain him for a century, he thought. He could go on for a long time, indeed, taking painful bites from the flesh of his creation.

‡

One night, late in summer, the apples were heavy again on the branches. When Baltasar summoned the golem to the glow of witchlight, when he seized her chin in his hand and looked into her eyes, she looked back.

Plainly and frankly, she looked back.

Fixedly and certainly, she looked back.

She was a flesh thing now, he realized. Not an apple thing.

And slowly she opened her jaw, curled back her lips, and Baltasar saw that the inside of her mouth was pink and lined with row after row of teeth. Tiny, white teeth.

Her hands closed around his wrist. She had a strength he had not guessed at. She had never resisted him.

"No!" he said, but the word was only a word, for she was no longer what she had been, and before he could summon the other words he knew, the ones that might destroy her even if he could not control her, she was bending toward him for a kiss. A very hungry kiss.

‡

What binds one may bind the other.

Bruce Holland Rogers

‡

Day by day, she called to him. Day by day, he was compelled to come to her from his place among the apple trees and submit. For a time, he still had a will of his own, still remembered the words that might release him, but he could not speak them. He had no tongue.

‡

There are still places where no one goes. Perhaps, one day, wandering in the woods, you will go to one of them. Losing your way, you will find yourself in deeper and deeper forest, and then find a little clearing where apple trees grow wild and bear their hard and bitter fruit. A stone hut stands there. Perhaps you will knock and find the woman who lives there. If she smiles, it will be a tight-lipped smile. She will not speak. Most likely, she will not answer your knock at all.

Out of the corner of your eye, you may see something moving beneath the tangled apple branches. Look fast enough, and you will glimpse a thing that you will be sure you cannot have really seen.

But if you were sure you had, indeed, seen it, and if you wanted a name for it, you could call it this: bone golem.

It had another name once, but that was long ago.

‡

Das ist die alte, alte Liebesgeschichte:
This is the old, old story of love.

Wind over Heaven

Coming into the restaurant early one Monday morning, Eric found Sutherland in the main dining room. One of Sutherland's massive arms rested casually, heavily on the open door of an antique china cabinet, and Eric could imagine the delicate hinges tearing out of the wood. Sutherland was examining the porcelain inside. No one had touched those porcelain pieces since Eric's mother had died and he had inherited them.

"What are you doing here?" Eric said.

Sutherland smiled. In the full moon of his face, the smile seemed tiny, as if his mouth were two sizes too small for him. "Hello, partner," he said. He handled the porcelain casually, turning the pieces over as if looking for a price sticker. When he picked up a little gold-rimmed demitasse, there was a moment when Eric imagined he was going to swallow it.

Eric stepped forward, took the demitasse from Sutherland's doughy hands. "This cabinet's supposed to be locked," he said.

"It was locked," Sutherland said. "I found the key in your office. You know, Eric, antiques aren't exactly an efficient use of capital. You could decorate a lot less expensively."

Eric felt the heat rise in his face. "In the first place, how the restaurant is decorated is part of what makes it a success. And in the second place, those pieces are part of my personal collection."

Sutherland smiled again. "Come on, Eric. You can't start sheltering assets after the fact. If it's in the restaurant, it's part of the restaurant. I think we need to talk about how we can cut overhead, reallocate our resources. If we make full use of all of our equity—" He reached into the cabinet and removed the demitasse. "—then maybe we can get this cash flow turned around."

"You want a court fight."

"Of course not. That would ruin The Tarragon Leaf, put a lot of people out of work. I just want to run an efficient business. Maybe if we can't agree on that, you should let me buy you out. You could start fresh somewhere else."

Eric said nothing. He was thinking about Sutherland's neck, about how it would be impossible to get one's hands all the way around it. You'd need a rope. Or piano wire.

"Here's my offer," Sutherland said, "and, believe me, it's better than your recent numbers warrant. I'm being generous."

‡

In the kitchen, after Sutherland had left, it was quiet. Monday mornings were always quiet, since The Tarragon Leaf wouldn't serve dinner again until Tuesday evening. Eric had thought that this would be a good time to come in and think about things, a time when he could expect Sutherland *not* to be in the restaurant.

Now, at least, he and Gero had the kitchen to themselves, and Eric, watching the stove's blue flame, could hear the hiss of the gas.

"Sutherland's a parasite," Eric said. "Why didn't I see that before it was too late?"

"Parasite," Gero said. He turned up the flame. "You think that is bad."

Eric forced a laugh. "Could it possibly be good?"

Gero didn't answer immediately. He was searching among the unlabeled jars that cluttered his shelves. When he squinted, the Asian slant of his gray eyes was more pronounced than usual. The water in the saucepan began to boil vigorously, but Gero ignored it until he had found what he was looking for — a jar of bright yellow powder that was probably mustard. But perhaps not. On those rare occasions when Gero wasn't in the restaurant, Eric would sometimes examine the contents of the jars, sniffing this, tasting a pinch of that. Some of the ingredients were spices that he recognized, but many of them remained mysteries. Gero's stock of ingredients was like his ethnicity — exotic and impossible to name.

Gero turned the flame back down, tapped some of the yellow powder into the water, then pulled at his reddish Magyar mustache as he searched through the jars again.

"Some parasites, you would not *choose* them," he said, "but once you have them . . ." He shrugged. "In Thailand there is a pickled fish that is so white, so firm." He kissed his fingertips. "You want to taste things. At least once. Well, this fish has a price for tasting. In his flesh, there are cysts. Tiny. Once you eat, the cysts break, and in your liver, in a little while, there are worms. Maybe in *my* liver. I don't know. Just a few are no trouble."

Gero's accent, Eric decided, sounded Russian today. Slavic, anyway. But it could shift. Sometimes it sounded Chinese.

Gero was showing Eric his smallest fingernail. "Not even that big, these worms. Flat, like that. I just eat the fish one time, no problem. Parasites are not so bad, then. Everything is balance, yes? I keep explaining to you. *Balance.*"

"Balance, right," Eric said. "Every time we have one of our little business dinners, Sutherland hits me with another surprise. But I should find some way to *balance* him. Sure."

Gero took down another jar. This one contained a woody root suspended in alcohol. It looked like a smaller version of the roots that Gero had hanging from the ceiling, up there with a wreath of bay leaves, the long strings of peppers, and the bunches of bulbs that looked like garlic, but weren't. Gero spooned a little of the alcohol into the boiling water and re-sealed the jar.

"You are impatient," Gero said. "When you are sick, you think only of cures."

"Well, of course!"

"First you must think of the sickness. Its nature."

"Okay, look," Eric said, "so maybe parasite isn't the right word for him."

"Sounds perfect," Gero said. "Business is good like always, but something is happening to money. Poof." He was adding a pinch from this jar and a pinch from that one to the boiling water. He turned down the heat. "Your partner is like tapeworm. Restaurant brings in same as before, but is getting skinny. How skinny? Little bit isn't bad. Most people, if they have tapeworm, they don't know it. Tapeworm isn't so bad."

"What I'm talking about," Eric said, "is embezzlement. Mismanagement. All these decisions he forces down my throat."

"And what *I* am talking about," Gero said, "is balance." He strained the contents of the saucepan through a paper filter into a ceramic carafe. "Wind over heaven."

"What?"

Gero tapped one of the Chinese books stacked next to his jars. "The ninth hexagram is wind above, heaven below. The Taming Power of Small Things. This is no time to act. Be subtle. Observe. Seek balance." Gero poured a few ounces of the amber infusion into a teacup. "You are agitated. Too much worry is too much bile. Drink this."

Eric opened his mouth to speak, then closed it. He accepted the cup with a sigh. It was no use trying to decline Gero's remedies. Gero would pester him until he drank it. In any case, the brews seemed harmless enough.

"Be patient," Gero said. "Don't make another mistake. He is your partner, now, and that was your choice. Now you want him out. What do you have to do to get him out? If you have a tapeworm, you must take poison enough to kill tapeworm, but not to kill you. How much poison must Tarragon Leaf swallow to get rid of this partner? How sick you are going to make my restaurant?"

Eric sipped the concoction. It was slightly bitter, but not bad.

My restaurant, Gero called it. Technically, it was Eric's restaurant. Well, Eric's and Sutherland's, now. But Gero was right in a way.

‡

There were times, Eric thought, when it all seemed a little surreal. Twelve years ago, when The Tarragon Leaf was struggling in its infancy, when Eric had a splendid atmosphere to go with not-yet-splendid food, Gero had shown up. Two days earlier, the original saucier had quit. Clutching a battered satchel, Gero was vague about his training and references, and his accent that day was generic pidgin. "I know sauce," he said. "I know food. Let me show."

What the hell, Eric had thought. He picked three sauces from the menu — a cerleriac rémoulade, a lobster chiffonade, and béarnaise. "Make these."

In the kitchen, Gero looked over the spice racks, muttering and shaking his head. Eventually, he opened the satchel and set its contents on the counter — jars of dried powders, roots, mushrooms. There were two books, too, their leather covers stamped in gold with Chinese characters. But Gero didn't consult these. He worked by tasting his base, adding an infinitesimal trace of some powder or another, and tasting the base again, so that he was absurdly slow, and Eric already knew the answer would be no, sorry, we have no position for you.

Until he tasted the finished sauces.

They weren't what the restaurant had ever served before. They weren't, Eric was almost certain, what *any* restaurant had served before. It seemed like magic.

"Not magic," Gero said. "*Balance.*"

His sense of balance, as it turned out, extended to more than sauces. Though he always insisted that he was a saucier and only a saucier, he was soon giving advice to others in the kitchen about everything from perfectly timed créme patissière to deftly positioned garnish. He was subtle about it. Balanced, you could say. He managed to offer compliments that planted only the tiniest hint

Bruce Holland Rogers

of dissatisfaction, the barest clue that he had available some advice to offer about how something that was nearly perfect could be nearer still.

And if Gero's area in the kitchen grew a little strange, with its drying herbs and spices hanging here and there, its unlabeled jars filled with the unknown, if it became, in fact, a little spooky on the days when his suppliers — often speaking no English — appeared in the kitchen with jars wrapped in brown paper, that was easy enough to overlook. The food, the reputation, the growing success of The Tarragon Leaf more than made up for the dreamlike witchiness of the saucier's shelves.

Besides, Eric liked the man. How could he fail to like him? The Tarragon Leaf had been Eric's dream, but it seemed that Gero dreamed it, too. He was nearly always there, even on Mondays, rearranging his things in the kitchen, experimenting, and often giving Eric a taste of something new, something divine.

Sometimes the herbal remedies that Gero dispensed for imaginary maladies he had diagnosed as "bad humors" or "overbearing yang" were a little hard to swallow. But they seemed a small price to pay.

‡

The table in The Tarragon Leaf's private dining room wasn't small, but Spencer Sutherland's bulk at one end made it seem that way to Eric. "There are certain economies we need around here," Sutherland way saying, his words muffled by a mouthful of salad.

Eric said, "What do you mean?"

Sutherland swallowed. "Like this salad." He took a bite that was too big and chewed it impatiently. Eric wished that he'd paid attention to how Sutherland ate before he had agreed to the marriage of their restaurants. Sutherland's first bite of anything would be careful. He would consider as he chewed. Then, once he had passed judgement, he would eat the rest too fast to savor. Once he knew what something was, he ate only to absorb, to acquire.

"What about the salad?" It was Belgian endive and fennel, with a very light vinaigrette, a palate-clearing course between appetizer and main course.

"We're importing this endive." Sutherland took another wolfish bite. Eric had hardly started on his own salad, and Sutherland's was nearly gone. "I mean, it's salad, Eric. And you're ordering from Europe? They grow this stuff in California, now. Cheap."

"It's called Belgian endive for a reason." Eric pointed with his fork. "See how the stalk has this closed shape? Around Brussels, they grow it underground, in heated soil. Growers in California don't take the same care."

"I know all that," Sutherland said. "But it tastes the same."

"The presentation is different."

Sutherland rolled his eyes.

"The reason this restaurant has the reputation it does," Eric said, "is that we take pains with detail."

"Yeah, well, it's a little hard to keep up with detail that you can't pay for." Sutherland pushed his plate aside. "I mean, you want to keep The Tarragon Leaf afloat, right?"

Eric's jaw clenched. "We're doing as much volume as ever," he said. "I don't see where this cash crunch has come from, unless you're doing less business at Southern Exposure."

"My place is doing fine," Sutherland said. He always spoke about The Tarragon Leaf as *our* restaurant and the Southern Exposure as *mine*, Eric realized. That wasn't the only inequality. He insisted on changes for The Tarragon Leaf, but wouldn't listen to the suggestions Eric had made for Sutherland's Southern Exposure steakhouse. The partnership was supposed to be collaborative. Advisory. At least that's how they had talked it out before signing the papers.

"You've got to understand," Sutherland was saying, "that there are certain administrative costs built in to the partnership."

"This merger was supposed to save us money. Both of us."

"And it will, eventually," Sutherland said. "Look, you yourself admitted to me that accounting issues weren't your strong suit, right? That's why we're in business together, to benefit from each others' strengths."

How could Eric *ever* have trusted him enough to tell him that money was the one thing he had trouble with? Not that there wasn't plenty coming in. The Tarragon Leaf was a success by any measure. But Eric had always found keeping track of money such a headache. It was the food he cared about. The food, the presentation, the atmosphere . . .

"It'll be all right. Trust me on that. But for now, I'm trimming your budget."

"Trimming my budget?" Eric said. "You can't do that!"

"Eric, read the agreements. You're in charge of operations. I'm in charge of budget and accounting. If you don't like it, sell out to me. You've heard my offer."

Eric's hand closed around a butter knife. He brandished it, then looked at it and put it down. "I'm bringing in an auditor."

Sutherland froze for half a second. He looked at Eric as if reappraising him. "You can't do it. We can't spend on something like that. We have to *economize*."

"I can do it. I am doing it."

"Eric," Sutherland said, "we're *partners*." He shrugged. "But I see you're going to insist. All right. At least pick someone good."

"I have. His name is Webber."

"Richard Webber?" Sutherland's teeth were big and white when he smiled. "I know Dick. He'll do a fine job. A fine job. Then you'll feel better. And you'll see that I'm right about cutting back a little, just temporarily. To keep us in the black." Sutherland lifted his wineglass and drained it. "Where's that waiter with the next course?"

‡

The dinner rush had begun, and Gero had the makings for three white sauces started in three different pans. In a fourth saucepan was an inch or so of mud-colored water. Eric watched it bubble. "That audit was a waste of money," he said.

"You don't trust the accountant?" Gero said, stirring and tasting each sauce in succession. He opened a jar.

"I trust the one I finally hired," Eric said, "the one who Sutherland didn't know. But he couldn't find anything." Actually, that wasn't entirely true. The auditor had made a stink about the records for Gero's purchases of ingredients. The saucier's suppliers did not furnish adequate invoices. Sutherland, with obvious pleasure, was insisting that Eric do something about this, but Eric wasn't up to broaching the subject with Gero now.

"Your kidneys are rising."

"Rising kidneys," Eric said. That could only mean that the roiling liquid on the stove was intended for him.

Gero tossed a whole mushroom onto the oily surface and cut the flame. The he stirred the sauces again. "So the partner, he is an honest man," Gero said. "Not parasite. Something else."

"No. I know he's pulling something, but he's clever. And he *knows* he's clever. God, I hate that smile of his."

"Parasites are not always bad. I told you. Tarragon Leaf can have a parasite and still be Tarragon Leaf."

"It's not just the embezzlement, Gero. He keeps insisting that I cut expenses, buy cheaper ingredients . . ."

Gero looked up. "Cheap? He wants you to buy cheap for Tarragon Leaf?" Gero shook his head. "To have the best is expensive."

"Yes."

"If it is not the best, is not Tarragon Leaf."

"That's how I feel about it. He'll bleed us to death. Bit by bit, we'll give up little pieces of what we do, and the restaurant won't be The Tarragon Leaf anymore."

"So he *is* a parasite, this partner." Gero started straining the liquid. "Still," he said, "if we are patient, he will learn. He will not be so bad."

Eric didn't think that was likely.

"If he doesn't learn, end the partnership."

"The only way to do that is to buy him out," Eric said. "I don't have the money. Especially now. He's going to ruin me. I can feel it."

"Smart parasite does not kill his host."

"Not all parasites understand that, Gero."

"Kidneys are rising," Gero said, handing him a steaming cup. "Drink."

Eric sipped the steaming brew. Whether his kidneys fell back into place or not, he couldn't tell. In any case, he didn't feel any better about the prospects for his restaurant.

‡

"I'd take a big loss, selling," Eric told Gero. It was a Monday morning again, and they were alone, watching water simmer in a pan. "But I probably can't get more out of him than he's offering, and the partnership agreement ties my hands. But it's not a dead loss. I'm thinking we can start over. Sutherland insists on a non-competing covenant, so we'd have to move to another city. It'd have to be a small restaurant to begin with, but I'd take along any staff who want to make the move . . ."

"Not me," the saucier said. "I will not leave Tarragon Leaf."

Eric didn't know what to say. Finally, he told Gero, "It won't *be* The Tarragon Leaf, even if you stay."

"Listen for example," said Gero. "You have a good friend. You are always together drinking, talking. You love this friend like your brother. Like twin. You are balancing to each other. Understand? Then he gets sick. He changes. He is not so interesting, always sick. So, Eric, you leave him? When he needs you?"

The saucier looked at his arrays of jars, then shook his head. "If you are thinking like this, the problem is your heart. Bad faith. There is no medicine I can give you for it." He turned off the burner and poured the steaming water down the sink.

"Well what would you suggest, exactly?" Eric said. "I don't have a lot of options."

"Patience. Let me think. It's a matter of balance. Suppose you are right, and he is a bad parasite. A bladder worm. You know bladder worm?"

Eric shook his head.

Bruce Holland Rogers

"Tapeworm babies," Gero said. "Larva. They hatch from eggs inside your stomach, dig into intestine walls, then into blood, yes? All through your body, even your brain. In a few years, they start to die. Dead ones swell up in your brain like little balloons."

Eric rubbed at his temples. Dead worms in the brain. He thought of Swiss cheese. He felt a headache coming on. "And then what?"

Gero made a gesture of expansion with his hands. "Pressure in brain. Epilepsy, shaking, fits. Maybe, you die. But you don't know about these worms until too late. That is what kind of parasite you selected to be your partner. Now we know what he is, but Tarragon Leaf already swallowed him."

Eric had a fleeting vision of Sutherland as an enormous worm. He felt sick. "If this is supposed to make me more hopeful," Eric said, "it isn't working."

"You are not going to sell the restaurant. We do not abandon sick friend."

"I don't know," Eric said. "If Sutherland is a bladder worm, I think our sick friend may be terminal."

‡

Although Eric was filled with thoughts of doom, the restaurant was hardly showing symptoms. Eric knew that would change. He concentrated on running the dining room and avoiding Spencer Sutherland when Sutherland tried to see him.

Finally, after a week of this, Eric took one of Sutherland's calls. "A house divided against itself cannot stand," Sutherland said. "Let's have a meeting over dinner. Get your boys to broil us some steaks. I like mine well done."

"Every time we talk," Eric said, "it's bad news. I don't want to hear any more."

"I'm going to make it worth your while," Sutherland said. "And if you ignore me, I can make it hurt. Read your contracts. I can just about close you down."

‡

In the kitchen before the meeting, Gero said, "Drink this."

For once it was a cold concoction, not a steaming one.

"What do I have?" Eric said. "High kidneys? Rising yin?"

"Heart problem still," said Gero. "Bad faith. You are thinking of selling." While they talked, he was making two sauces. Two brown sauces. Around them was the usual kitchen racket, but it wasn't up to its frantic pace. The evening was early, and the restaurant wasn't yet half full. "You will not sell, all right?"

"Depends on what he offers."

"Drink."

Eric took a sip, then made a face. Of all the brews Gero had ever made for him, this was the worst. "Are you poisoning me?"

Gero looked up, his gray eyes thoughtful. "That would keep you from selling?"

"Sutherland would still get the restaurant."

"Then what is the advantage to poisoning you? Drink. You are having serious bad faith. It's getting worse, I think."

Eric held his breath and drank the stuff. There was grit at the bottom of the glass.

"Let this partner offer you the moon and stars," Gero said. "Don't sell before you talk to me." He turned back to the stove. "I am making a wonderful sauce for the steak tonight. Something new."

"We can't . . ." Eric looked around the kitchen, then lowered his voice. "We can't poison him. Don't think I haven't thought about it, but we'd never get away with it."

"We need balance," Gero said. "Takes time. You are going to be patient. Meet with your partner, enjoy a good dinner. *Relax.*"

‡

Dinner should not have been relaxing, but it was. By the time the main course had come, Eric was, if not in a state of bliss, at least profoundly calm. A little sleepy, in fact. He could not have said why. Certainly, Sutherland's eating habits hadn't suddenly improved. There was nothing calming about seeing the man belt down his appetizer and salad after only one preliminary, appraising bite of each.

The steaks arrived — well-done for Sutherland, rare for Eric. The waiter put them down wrong initially, and Sutherland started cutting into his. "Hey," he said, "I like mine cooked!"

The waiter apologized and exchanged the plates. Then Eric watched as Sutherland cut one modest bite. "Oh, this is marvelous," he said. "Perfectly marbled. It melts."

"So that's one thing you think I'm doing right," Eric mumbled.

Sutherland laughed. "Not at all," he said. "Serving this to your customers squeezes your margin. I can get almost as good for considerably less. I think both restaurants ought to use the same meat supplier."

He carved his next bite, an enormous chunk that he hardly chewed before swallowing. Eric supposed that Sutherland's choking to death was too much to hope for.

At least Eric had the satisfaction of enjoying Gero's steak sauce. It was nouvelle Mexican, a sort of *mole*, but lighter on salt than one would expect. There was more chile than chocolate, and on the whole it had Gero's distinctive *wholeness*. It was, as Gero would say, balanced. But Sutherland probably wasn't even tasting it any more.

As soon as he'd swallowed the last piece of meat, Sutherland reached into his pocket for a packet of folded papers. "I'm making you a take it or leave it deal," he said. "Better price than before. We want to resolve this, right? I think it's too late to mend fences."

Eric glared.

The price Sutherland quoted was an improvement. He shoved the papers across the table for Eric to look at.

"All in all, this is simply an unfortunate falling out," Sutherland said. "It happens sometimes." He offered Eric a pen.

‡

Gero had another glass for him like the earlier one, but Eric refused to drink it.

"Is better if you do drink," Gero said.

"Forget that," Eric said. He unfolded the papers. "Everything's drawn up already, see? He's eager to be rid of me. That increased the price."

"You signed?" Gero said.

"You said I should talk to you first," Eric told him, "so I'm talking. But it's a better deal. Enough better that I'm thinking *you* might reconsider. Gero, think about the struggle it would be here, to hold together a restaurant while Sutherland is trying to break it up into little pieces he can sell."

"I will not go."

"Well I might." Eric held out the papers. "I *will*."

"You are forgetting your friend who is sick. You are turning your back on Tarragon Leaf."

"Gero, The Tarragon Leaf is a terminal case. Whether I stay or go, Sutherland is in the picture, and that means that the restaurant you and I know is already history. He's a bladder worm, remember?"

"Ah, yes. A bladder worm," Gero said. "Better you drink this." He offered the noxious drink again.

"Look, forget that nonsense," Eric said. He picked up the drink, walked it to the sink, and poured it out.

Gero took a deep breath. That was the most extreme expression of exasperation Eric had ever seen him make. "All right," Gero said, "I will show you."

He looked around the kitchen. It was late, but the other chefs, the pot scrubbers, the dish washers were all still busy. No one seemed to be paying particular attention to the conversation. "Restaurant has a parasite," Gero said very quietly. "What is a better treatment for parasite than another parasite?" He produced a jar. Inside was something that looked like a long, curled shaving of wax. Even without knowing what it was, there was something about its appearance that made Eric's stomach turn.

Gero tapped the side of the jar. "Tapeworm pieces," he said. "Proglottids. Fresh. Ripe. Full of eggs." He reached among his jars and produced a second and third jar with similar contents.

Eric thought he felt something twitch in his intestines. The kitchen air suddenly seemed very stale.

"I had to get several. I had to make sure I would have many eggs. It must be a big infection to make sure the bladder worms get to the brain."

"Where . . ."

"From Mexico, from pigs," Gero said. "I have sources, yes? I tell them it must be fresh."

"But I mean, where . . ."

"In the steak sauce, remember? In your partner's steak sauce, not yours. The eggs are too small to see, though, so I worry, just a little sauce on a spoon is bad. Or the waiter makes mistake."

"Bad. Yes." And the waiter *had* made a mistake. Had Eric's steak knife perhaps touched the sauce on Sutherland's steak? He tried to remember. Surely, if there were bladder worm larvae in Eric's stomach, he couldn't *feel* them. Surely that crawling sensation was his imagination.

"But now, all we need is patience," Gero went on. "In four years, your partner will not be running any restaurant. Maybe we will buy Southern Exposure. We will make two fine restaurants then, Eric. With balance." He smiled. There was light in his gray, Sino-Ugrian-Russo-Mediterranean eyes. "What did I tell you? Wind over heaven. The Taming Power of Small Things. Your partner is a man out of balance. Big body, big appetite, very big greed. With something small, now, we tame him."

"The drink," Eric said. His mouth felt dry. "Some kind of herbs?"

Gero shook his head. "Herbs for some things, for subtle things, are fine. But for killing worms, making sure you are not infected, we need the best poison. Quinacrine hydrochloride. Makes you vomit sometimes, so I put in some catnip and phenobarbital. I will make you another now."

Eric, still looking at the worm pieces in the jars, thought he saw one move. He rushed to the sink and leaned forward.

Gero stood watching him for a moment. "Recipe is not balanced," he said. "I think, this time, more phenobarbital."

Eric rose to breathe, then leaned forward again.

Gero sighed and shook his head. "It is difficult. This is not something I can balance by taste." He opened a jar full of pills, and he shrugged.

"After all," he said, "I am not a doctor. I am only a saucier."

Bright Seeds in a Whirlwind

Because she was always working when the shows were on, Petra never got to watch the telenovelas in their entirety. She was alone in the Reyes y Tejada house on Thursdays, and she could turn up the sound in the living room and listen to *With All My Heart* while she scrubbed the kitchen floor. Over Señora Lerma's shoulder, she could catch a scene or two of *Pearls and Stones* as she dusted. Sometimes when Señora Velarde was drinking her third sherry after lunch, she would say, "Come on, Petra! You can beat those rugs later. Come keep me company while *The End of Love* is on," and they would watch together, Señora Velarde sipping sherry and Petra drinking from a glass of water, like equals. But before the show was over, even if it looked like that no-good Faqueza was finally about to get her comeuppance, Petra would have to return to the rugs. If she didn't, she'd be late getting halfway across Mexico City to Señora Galindo's house, where last time in her haste she had neglected to sweep the courtyard and could only hope that the Señora hadn't noticed.

The betrayals, scheming, and true love of the telenovelas gave her something to think about instead of wondering where Diego's father had gone off to. At the Sonora Market, she bought a candle for Visions of the Missing, but when she burned it, she saw nothing. She didn't even dream of him. Then, on *With All My Heart*, poor Norberto was killed in a car crash, leaving Andeana to raise their son alone. The next time someone asked, Petra reported her "husband's" death in just such an accident. "I only hope that he felt no pain," she added. That's what the heartbroken Andeana had said about Norberto before she dissolved into tears.

Evenings, when she returned to her room in the vecindad, Petra would collect Diego from the neighbor who watched him. "He's an angel," the neighbor would say. "At four, they can be demons, but he's very quiet."

At first, Petra had agreed that a quiet child was a blessing. But as time went on, she began to worry that Diego's silences might be a sign of idiocy or madness. He would stare for a long time at nothing at all, and often when he did say two sentences together, it was to report things that had not happened.

"Those boys, they were picking fruit out of the tree. And they ate it."

"What boys? What are you talking about?"

"In the courtyard. That tree with the fruit like big strawberries, the boys climbed it."

"Diego, don't talk nonsense. There's no tree in the courtyard."

"It's not there now," he said. "Just sometimes."

She burned a candle for the Virgin of Guadalupe every night, in case that should help. But it only gave her light by which to see how many times Diego sat up in his cot during the night, wide-eyed, staring at the walls.

"Diego, go to sleep."

"They're fighting! They're cutting their legs!"

"You're having a dream."

He lay back down, but did not close his eyes for a long time. Petra watched him until she fell asleep, only to be awakened by his sobbing. "They took the hurt ones away. Now they will cut their hearts. I've seen it!"

On Sunday, she took him to a curandera who lived in a room without windows. The old woman touched Diego all over with her yellow fingers. She sprinkled some powder on his shoulders, on his head. She blew a tiny bit into his eyes, which made them water. Then she lit some more of her candles.

"Now, boy, tell me the truth," the curandera said. "Do you see things other people can't see?"

Diego looked at his mother and nodded shyly.

"What do you see?"

"I saw the men fighting. They had clubs with black teeth in them. For cutting the legs." He sawed at his own leg with his hand.

"Diego — " said Petra.

The curandera waved her to silence.

"How were they dressed?"

"Like birds. They had feathers."

"Ah. What else have you seen?"

"I saw a lady buy a hat with feathers."

"The hat had feathers? What kind of feathers?"

"No. I mean, she gave the man feathers and he gave her the hat.

Most of them were green. There were some red ones and some blue ones."

"You're telling me the truth?"

Diego nodded. "And I hear things, too. I heard the wind talk. It said, 'Tsikay daineuzlatl.' That means, 'I am your breath.'"

"Ay!"

"What? Is that Nahuatl? Is it a real language?" Petra's eyes were wide.

"No," said the curandera, "not Nahuatl. But it sounds like it, doesn't it?" The curandera snipped a thatch of hair from the boy's head. With his hand, Diego felt the bristly spot.

"Is he lying?" asked Petra. "Is it a curse? Is he possessed?"

"Let's see, let's see," the curandera said. She sifted the hair between her fingers, so that it fell in patterns onto a page of newspaper. Then she brought the candles close to read what the hair told her. For a long time, she remained in silent study.

"What visions!" the old woman said at last. "It is a dream that your son dreams. A true dream. He sees visions of a world, another fold of creation. It is a true world that does not exist."

Petra said, "How can that be?"

The curandera moved the candles, then she laughed. "I don't know, but that's what I see. It is like a miracle!"

"It's good for his future, then?" Petra said. Her hands wrung the corner of her blouse. "I have certain hopes."

The curandera moved the candles again. "I think he might be very wise. Yes, the things he sees in the other world will teach him." She looked at Diego. "For you, God opens a window that is closed to the rest of us."

"Yes," said Petra, "but what sort of life — "

"His wisdom will not be visible to most. But a few will know him for what he is. For them, for *us*, you are a gift, Diego!"

The boy blinked, said nothing.

"Yes, but his prospects —"

"Work will avoid him. Money will never stick to him. I think . . . I think he will be one of those men who sleeps in the park. His eyes will watch the other world."

"Mother of God. I can't let that happen!"

"My dear, it is your son's destiny." She prodded the hairs on the newspaper. "He will not be unhappy."

"You don't understand. You don't understand. I will wear myself out raising him. I'm saving money for his schooling."

"He is getting his schooling already, aren't you, Diego?"

"It has to be undone!" Petra cried. "These visions, these dreams, they have to be stopped!"

"That would be dangerous," said the curandera. She began to blow out candles.

"But you know a way? Can you cure him?"

"It would be no cure. Don't you see that he is bound to this other world? You would be cutting out a piece of him. He's important. You would be tampering with — "

"But it can be done, yes?"

The curandera lifted a white taper. "No," she said. She looked at Diego, at the tiny candle flames in his eyes. "Not by me. Not by the likes of me."

‡

In the Sonora Market, there were stalls where all the candles sold were black, except for the tall vigil candles in red glasses marked Death Against My Enemies or Evil Eye Unblinking. In these stalls Petra asked, and asked again, until she found someone who would teach her the spell and sell her the ingredients.

She woke herself at three in the morning, took Diego by the hand, and led him into the narrow courtyard of the vecinidad. As if breathing, the ghostly shapes of drying laundry stirred against the stars. Diego clutched his bare chest and shivered as Petra lit the black candle. It was in the shape of an owl, and she perched it in a hole in the concrete where it would be out of the breeze. She poured water into the wide pail that served the children as a bath. "Get in. Now sit down."

"Mama, it's cold."

"It's cold sleeping the the park, too. You'll have a better life this way. It's for your sake that I'm doing this." She pushed him down into the water, soaking his underpants. Diego cried.

"Shh! You'll wake someone." She poured scooped water in a bowl and poured it over his head. He whimpered, and she seized his chin. "Silence!"

She cut her thumb with the razor. The ointment had hardened in its little jar, and it wasn't softened much by the drops of blood she added. Petra dug the ointment out with her finger and had to press very hard to paint Diego's skin with it. He flinched, but he didn't make another sound, except to say, "It stinks."

Around her son's neck she painted a shirt collar. On his collarbone, she made a triangle for the knot of a necktie, then painted the tie down to his navel. "Diego Deverez, my son, here is your destiny," she said. She painted his chest with lapels. "You are going to go to school and learn your numbers. You are going to learn English."

Bruce Holland Rogers

She painted pockets for the suit. She pressed his wrist bones hard to smear on buttons for his cuffs. "You will get a job in a bank, where you will work hard and make lots of money." She painted a peso sign on each palm. Then she took him by the shoulders.

"I'll give you some savings, and we'll buy a nice house in Satellite City. You'll take care of your mama, and you'll never, ever leave her. This is your dream, now. This is our dream together."

She pulled out two of her hairs by the roots. One she tied, like a choker, around Diego's throat. That was difficult. The ends were hard to see in the dark. Even harder was tying the other hair around her own neck. She couldn't see what she was doing, and she had to start over again several times while Diego sat shivering.

"For your sake," she said to him again.

She scooped more water over his head, then scrubbed him with black soap and a stone until the ointment was rubbed so deep that it couldn't be seen. She dried him off, blew out the candle. Under the electric light of their room, his skin was red and raw. He cried again, and she let him. "Go to sleep," she said, "and dream about the nice house we're going to have in Satellite City."

In the morning the hairs were gone.

She repeated the ritual for the next two nights, then left the black owl burning when she went to work. By the time she came home, it had consumed itself.

Now, she thought, we'll see.

‡

Atalaya Malacatl's legs ached because she'd been kneeling for so many hours at the front of the church. It would feel so good to stand, but fear kept her on her knees.

For years, Atalaya had been coming to the little church of Our Lady of the Waters to kneel before its Jesucristo. In churches closer to the shack where she lived with her daughter, there were also Jesucristos nailed to their crosses and bleeding from their many wounds. But here, Our Lord revealed himself differently. Elsewhere his face showed only his agony. Here, though his flesh was drained to whiteness and his hands were curled like claws around the nails, he looked out upon his torturers with eyes that were gentle. He was being murdered, and he didn't hate anybody.

That, decided Atalaya the first time that she saw him, was miracle enough. She began to take the bus here for every Mass.

Soon after, the White Jesucristo began coming to her in dreams. Before then she would pray often to the Blessed Virgin for help raising her daughter. Little Ignacia was dissatisfied with everything. It seemed as she grew, that she wanted to burn down the

121

whole world, and with the teachings from the Aztec codex, she might one day have the power to do just that. "Mary, intercede for me," she prayed. "Make my daughter more gentle."

The White Jesucristo appeared while she slept and told her that it was a sin to pray for anything in particular.

When she told a priest, he dismissed the dream, saying, "At the altar, we pray for things all the time." Between the teachings of a priest and Jesucristo himself, she knew whom to believe. She had to discover a new way of praying, and it was this: She would say, "Ay, Jesucristo, Jesucristo, Jesucristo," and she would think of how his eyes were gentle as he died upon the cross. Then he was with her, teaching her heart to be wounded, to be tender. And that was usually enough. She said it under her breath before she read the stars for someone. She said it when she needed to feel Jesucristo near.

Lately, she had been wistful for the old way of praying because things were getting worse with Ignacia. The girl was almost a woman, old enough to begin telling fortunes herself. But Ignacia was so angry, found so many things to hate. Lately it was the Spaniards. "They burned the codices, murdered the priests," Ignacia would say. "They stole the past! And then they brought a religion that thinks only of a future life. So here we are in the middle, in the present, connected to nothing at all." She complained about the city itself, about how crowded the buses were, how clogged the streets and sidewalks, how dirty the air. "Everything's gone wrong! Everything needs to change!"

Atalaya agreed that the world had gone wrong. But to fill one's heart with so much anger was dangerous. It was like praying in the wrong way — eventually it would turn against you.

So in recent weeks, she had prayed, "Ay, Jesucristo, Jesucristo. I am afraid for my daughter."

Then Atalaya began to hear rumors about Ignacia's visits to the Sonora Market. Her daughter had gone not into the stalls of the curanderos, but the ones where black candles were for sale. She'd been seen talking to certain people who knew certain things.

"We're astrologers! We don't meddle in that sort of thing," Atalaya had told her. "You must stop. I forbid it!"

Ignacia had given her such a scorching look that Atalaya crossed herself. That was why, today, she knelt before the White Jesucristo and said, "Ay, Jesucristo. I am afraid *of* my daughter. I have myself given her so much power, so much knowledge. It's not just myself that I fear for!"

Perhaps, Atalaya thought, she should have destroyed the Head of Heaven. She had promised her mother and grandmother to keep it safe, to teach its secrets to her own daughter. But perhaps such a thing should not even *be* in the world.

If she destroyed it, though, would she destroy the heavens? Would the world end utterly, with nothing to take its place? That would make Atalaya the murderer of the Fifth Sun.

"Ay," she prayed. "Jesucristo, Jesucristo, Jesucristo."

He gazed at her with his wooden eyes. If he was worried, he did not say so.

‡

Her son had a certain way of walking, and Petra Deverez could tell from the first heavy clomp of his shoes on the front steps that it wasn't some delivery man coming. But why was Diego home from work already? *He and She* was on, and Diego didn't usually arrive until after *The End of Love*. With the remote, she turned down the sound.

"What's wrong?" she said as he opened the door.

He laughed. "Nothing's wrong, mama. Look, I stopped on the way home and bought you a bottle of sherry. This is the kind you like, yes?"

"But you're home so early."

"I have some news."

News? She allowed herself to hope that it might involve a girlfriend. Let it be that. Yes, Diego could have been seeing her in secret. Her family disapproved, perhaps, but this was a love that could not be contained. Now the secret would come out. He had brought the sherry because she was coming to dinner.

"I've been promoted," he said. "I'll report directly to Garibaldi, the Vice President of the bank."

"Oh."

"Mama, you should be excited! We'll be able to pay down the mortgage on this house a lot faster. I'll buy you an even bigger television." He let his suit coat fall onto the couch.

"Your suit looks nice," she said. "You don't have to take it off the moment you come in."

Diego loosened his tie. "Mama, I wear that suit all day. It's heavy. It feels like I'm wearing armor all the time."

"Well hang it up at least. It will get wrinkled."

"Want me to pour you some sherry?"

She gestured at her glass. "I have some already."

"This is better. Imported." He sat down on the coffee table.

"Diego!"

He laughed, then said, "Mama, this promotion is a big deal."

Wind over Heaven

"You know what would be a big deal?" she said. "A girlfriend. A wedding. Some grandchildren."

"Garibaldi could be the bank's next president, you know, when Suárez retires. That's how they're talking. If Garibaldi moves up, I might move up with him."

Petra sighed. It was always like that with him if she mentioned romance. She said, "I don't know why it's always business and promotions. I don't know why you can't spend a little time thinking about a pretty girl who could give me a grandchild."

"Mama, I have you and you have me. That's all we need." He stood up. "Wait until you taste this sherry." He went into the kitchen.

On the television screen, Laurita and Adriano were kissing. They'd been about to fall in love for weeks, and now at last they were together. Why couldn't that happen for Diego? But Petra knew. It made her heart sink to think about it, but she knew. Petra hadn't dreamed a wife for him, or children.

It was her own fault.

‡

Only when his mother reminded him of it later did Diego Deverez think that the owl really might have been an omen. Her cries had sent him racing up the stairs to her bedroom where he found her clutching a pillow. She faced the window. The pane was cracked, and one of his mother's shoes lay on the floor near the sill.

"What happened?"

"Owl. Owl," she sobbed.

"An owl?" He hugged her. "Mama, don't be afraid. There aren't owls in the city. Where would they roost? And even if there were an owl around here, they're harmless unless you happen to be a mouse."

Her crying did not diminish, and Diego gave her his handkerchief. "It's all right, Mama. If you want, I'll go look for it. I'll scare it out of the neighborhood for good."

"It looked right at me. It's a sign," she said. "It's a bad omen."

He noticed how deep the lines in her face had become, how much gray there was in her hair. Omens and telenovelas. This was her life.

"What can I do?"

She caught her breath, wrung his kerchief in her hands. "Close the blinds, Diego."

The window glass would need replacing, but he didn't say anything about it. "Is that better?"

"Come sit with me."

Bruce Holland Rogers

He did, though he had some work to do that night. He stayed until she said that it was all right, that he could leave her. Later, while he worked at the kitchen table, he could hear her upstairs, coughing and coughing.

In the morning, when she came down for breakfast, Diego saw the pink stains on her handkerchief. "You're coughing blood!"

"I'll go to the Sonora Market," she said. "I'll see a curandero."

"A curandero. Maybe you should . . . Mama, I think you should see a *medical* doctor."

"I need a curandero, son. That's the sort of thing I have."

"We can afford both. I'll call the clinic and see if they can get you in tomorrow. I can take the afternoon off. I can take the afternoon off *today* if you like."

She insisted that a medical doctor would only waste their money, but he called and made an appointment for her anyway.

That day at work, he called her twice in the morning to hear her say that she was all right. The collar of his shirt itched, adding aggravation to his worry. He kept loosening his tie so he could scratch, but the irritation grew worse. In the washroom after lunch he opened his shirt to find that his neck was red from all the scratching.

He called home three times in the afternoon, but she was out every time. The itching got worse, and at the end of the day he went to the washroom again to find a thin ring of yellow in the redness. He picked at it and snagged a hair — no, three hairs twined together, wound all the way around his neck. When he had drawn them out of his skin, he stood over the sink for a long time, sickened, looking at them.

When he returned that evening, the house smelled like flowers and spices. On the coffee table between his mother and the television stood a row of aerosol cans. He picked one up. It was Essence of the Blessed Virgin. Another was Essence of Saint Francis.

"Did the curandero give you these, Mama?"

She shook her head. Her face was pale, her eyes red. "No. Not the curandero. I bought them at the Sonora Market. In her hands was a rosary.

"We'll go to the clinic tomorrow."

"It's no use," she said. She rubbed at the ring of red skin around her neck, which Diego had not noticed. Seeing it made his throat feel dry. "Witchery," she said. "By my own hand, says the curandero. There's nothing to do but prepare my soul." She put her hands to her face. "Diego, I'm so sorry! I thought it was right. To think of you sleeping in the park . . ."

125

Wind over Heaven

He knelt beside her. "What are you talking about? I'm not going to sleep in any park. Everything will be fine."

When she brought her hands away, her face was wet. "Spray some more of the Virgin," she said. "I want to feel her presence."

He felt embarrassed, but he did it for her.

"I have to admit that I was selfish," she said. "I said it was for you, Diego, but it was for *me*. Blessed Virgin, pray for me now and in the hour of my death."

"Mama, it's all right."

"No, I was selfish! For you, I told you. But I did it for myself. And now you have no wife, no children."

Diego felt her head, but her skin was cool. Even so, he insisted on helping her to bed. He set the saintly essences on her nightstand where she could reach them. Then he called the clinic and made them change the afternoon appointment to a morning one.

When the doctor at the clinic said that she should go immediately to the hospital, Petra said, "Do you see? By my own hand. God have mercy."

"Mama, you're going to get better," Diego promised. He brought the television from home and set it up in her hospital room. She watched it only for the first day. After that, she only picked at the bed clothes and would not answer when he spoke to her. She would look at him without seeming to know who he was.

"What does she have?" he asked the doctors. They said only that they needed to do more tests.

He took days off from work to be with her. After all, the nurses couldn't be checking every minute. By then Petra was getting oxygen through a tube, and if she tugged at the tube in her sleep and pushed it away, Diego could be right there to replace it. He wore his suit. That was how she liked to see him dressed.

She had one lucid moment when she sat up and looked at the window. "The owl," she said.

There was no owl, and he told her so. She looked at him as if perplexed, and her face softened. "Diego, it's you!" She let him take her hand. "That owl was an omen. You go to the Sonora Market, and you tell them what I did to you. I shouldn't have done it."

He stroked her hand. "You didn't do anything to me, Mama."

"I did!" She lay back down.

Toward morning, her breath became raspy. After listening to his mother's heart, the nurse told Diego that he should summon the priest.

Hours later, he stood in the hallway as the doctor said, "Almost certainly a cancer."

"She knew she was going to die." The sunlight at the end of the hall hurt Diego's eyes. "She expected it."

"We won't know the details for certain without an autopsy, but that's not necessary now."

"No," said Diego, feeling at his throat. "It's not."

‡

The world had dissolved. There were no more solid objects in it.

That's what he thought as the taxi took him up Paseo de la Reforma. Every monument and statue, every office building, every sidewalk cafe had a watery look to it.

It was late morning, but traffic was heavy. The taxi lurched ahead, then stopped.

The driver kept looking at him in the mirror, wondering, perhaps, if he was going to get paid. Diego kept changing his mind about where he wanted to go. In a world without substance, the simplest questions were impossible to answer. At the hospital, the driver had asked three times where he wanted to go.

"The park." It seemed to Diego that his voice came from the bottom of a lake, perhaps from the black waters on which the city floated.

"Which? Alameda?"

"Chapultepec." But when they got there, Diego couldn't remember why he had wanted to go there. They drove past the monument to the Boy Heroes, and Diego told the driver to circle the park, and then to drive up Reforma.

His suit coat felt unbearably heavy on his shoulders, but he lacked the strength to take it off. They passed the statue of Cuautémoc, the last Aztec Emperor, and something tugged at Diego's lungs. He almost remembered something. Almost. He felt a stab of nostalgia, but not for anything he could name.

They drove past the Columbus statue and the Spanish king on his horse. They kept going all the way to the Plaza of the Three Cultures and the ruins of the Tlatelolco pyramid. For a moment, he remembered a pyramid that he had seen in his childhood. Not a ruin, but a living temple. Men dressed as eagles stood in ranks upons its stones.

He blinked. When could he have seen such a thing?

"Take me home," he said, and gave the address.

When paid the driver, he found a green feather among the bills in his wallet.

His shoulders ached from the weight of the suit. As soon as he had let himself in, he let the coat drop to the floor. Without it, he suddenly felt dizzy. It wasn't the world that was becoming unsubstantial, he realized. It was him. He felt as if his bones were made of air.

‡

Diego slept all afternoon and all night. He dreamed of an Indian marketplace, and it was a strange dream because there was no story to it. There was just the buying and selling, hour after hour, in a language that Diego could barely understand. He woke to an impossible memory and a silent house. The memory was of a tree in the courtyard of his childhood vecinidad. The other boys were eating fruit from a strange tree. It was funny fruit, strawberries the size of apples. He wanted to taste it.

Diego stretched under the covers. The daylight in his room was . . . fresh. That was the best word. He could almost taste it.

A bell jangled. A telephone. The sound was bright and new. He got out of bed and was dizzy. His body felt light, and his feet hardly seemed to touch the floor. That made it hard to walk.

"Deverez," said the voice on the phone, "this is Espinel. I have some things I need to bring by for you, and I wanted to make sure you were home, eh."

"Señor Espinel," said Diego. "The man at the bank."

There was a pause. "Yes. You will be home for a while, eh? I'll be by in about an hour if the traffic isn't bad."

Diego looked out the window. The sky was brown. "It's very dirty today," he said. "The cars are making a real stink."

Another pause. "Well, an hour and a half then. See you then, okay?"

Diego hung up the phone and then noticed his suit coat lying on the floor. He wasn't supposed to leave it lying around like that, so he tried to pick it up. He couldn't. During the night, it had gotten too heavy to lift.

For breakfast he put sugar on his bread. No one was there to tell him not to. He ate some butter out of the dish. Then he went to see if being so light meant that he could run up the stairs faster. Actually, he was slower, because between steps he had to float back down.

If he kept getting lighter, he might float away from the world altogether, and that scared him. He got dressed and put all the coins he could find into his pants pockets. That might not be enough, so he put a brass candlestick in each pocket, too.

Señor Espinel came, and Diego let him in.

"There's no easy way to tell you this, don Diego," said Señor Espinel as he set down a box in Diego's living room. "Garibaldi

Bruce Holland Rogers

decided this morning to reorganize the departments, and, well, there isn't a position for you any more. We didn't know what would be better, under the circumstances, eh, with your mother's illness and all. Garibaldi said it might be easiest if you didn't have to come in. So he told me to bring the things from your desk."

"I got fired?"

"Well, no. It's a restructuring, eh? It's very sudden, I know."

Diego picked a glass paperweight out of the box. There was a flower inside. It was a lot prettier than he remembered.

"The timing is terrible, but Garibaldi thought later might be worse. How is your mother?"

"My mama is dead," Diego said.

Señor Espinel gave him a strange look. "My sincere condolences, don Diego. Most sincere. Most sincere, eh." Then he said, "Are you all right?"

Diego only nodded, because he knew he would cry if he tried to speak. Señor Espinel left, and Diego followed a few minutes later. He took a bus to the Zocalo. From there he walked to the Sonora Market. The smell of copal filled the air, sweeter than sugar or flowers. He could feel himself getting lighter and lighter as he looked at the bins labeled Indian Tea or Flower of Chance. Soon the candlesticks would not be enough to hold him down.

At the back of one stall, he saw a statue that was pretty big. Paying for it, he discovered another feather in his wallet. A blue one.

‡

When the man with the candlesticks in his pockets approached Ignacia Malacatl's folding table, she ignored him so she could go on dreaming her dream of transformation. How would this market be, in another world? She would want it to smell better — no orange peels rotting between the cobblestones. People would not be packed so tight that you had to snake your way through. Perhaps there would not be a market here at all, but a garden. Or a palace.

One of these days, she would know what replaced the crowded market. One of these days, she was going to know enough witchery, and she would use it to find the Empty One. After that, she wouldn't have to sit like a peasant in the market, giving astrological readings to people who *were* peasants. Everything, absolutely everything, would be different. And all the things Ignacia had done would be worth it. Even that business with her mother.

But to find the Empty One, Ignacia needed more witchery. To learn more witchery, she needed money. And the best way she knew how to make money was from what her mother had taught her, telling fortunes.

Señor Candlesticks gestured at the sign. "Excuse me," he said. "It says 'Divinations.'"

She looked him over. He was holding the fat Chinaman statue that Pilar Coreles has been trying to unload for a year.

"That's what it says," she admitted. The sign also said, *Your Future Revealed*. She puffed on her cigarette and squinted at the statue and its idiotic smile. It could stand for all the blandness of this world, for everything that needed changing. "That's a worthless piece of junk."

"It was the heaviest thing I could find," he said. "How do you do it?"

She exhaled smoke. "What?"

"How do you tell the future?"

"With the stars."

"Astrology."

She nodded. "But with the old stars. Not with Scorpio and Gemini. I watch Tepeyollotl, Tlaloc, Colotl Ixayac. The Mayan constellations, too. I peer into the smoke of creation."

He said, "I need to know something. How much?"

"Forty pesos for your lucky numbers. Sixty to answer a question about love or money."

"I want to know the future. What's to become of me?"

"For a comprehensive reading, a hundred and twenty pesos."

He had some difficulty opening his wallet, since he apparently didn't think of putting the statue down. She counted the money, folded it, and pinned it into her skirt.

"When were you born?" she asked as she opened her wooden box for the index cards. Her mother used to bring a handmade copy of the codex along to give readings, but one was liable to give away secrets that way. With the cards, Ignacia insured that no client saw more than a part of the Aztec sky.

He gave her the date. Eight Tooth, Nine Reed, Ten Jaguar, Eleven Bird . . . It took her a little while to count it out. "Six Lefthanded in Xiutecuhtli," she said, laying out the cards of the constellations and the stones that would help her keep track. "And your mother? Her birthday?"

He told her, and she counted again. "Eleven Rain in Cinteotl. What about your father?"

"I don't know about him."

"It's not as important," she said. Then she paused. There was something familiar about this configuration. Where had she seen it . . .

Her breath escaped her as if she'd been kicked. She looked at him, really *looked* at him. He was holding on to the edge of her table with one hand, as if he were afraid of floating away. In his eyes she saw a kind of openness that was strange for an adult. He was either an idiot, or . . .

Her hands shook as she started to put away the cards and counters, then stopped. "Wait. Let me make sure. Hold out your hand."

He set the statue gingerly on the table and, gripping the edge of the table more tightly, extended his other hand palm up. She turned his hand over and breathed three times on the glowing tip of her cigarette, then waved it hurriedly beneath his palm. Smoke tendrils seemed to pass right through his fingers.

"The Empty One," she said softly. Then, louder, "What's your name?"

"Diego," he said. "You're pretty." He was blushing.

She took a puff, then passed the cigarette beneath his hand again, this time with deliberate slowness. "No mistake," she said. "You are him."

"Am I going to keep getting lighter? I'm afraid I might float into the sky."

Could that really happen? That would explain why he gripped the table. Ignacia closed her hand around his wrist. "I'm sure not going to let you float away." She stood up and started to lead him out of the market. "I will help you, Diego. You have a destiny to fulfill."

"Where are we going?"

"We have to catch a bus."

"I don't like buses," he said. "Everyone pushes. Can we take a taxi?"

‡

The taxi took them through Coyoacan and Ixtapalapa, and as they drove, Diego recalled some of the bad things that he used to see — men cutting the legs out from other men, taking them for sacrifice. He was very quiet as Ignacia gave the driver directions, showed him where to turn onto the dirt road that went winding up the hill. After a while, the taxi stopped on the side of the hill.

"There's nothing here," Diego said.

"Down below," Ignacia told him. "I'll show you."

Diego opened his wallet to find nothing but colored feathers. Ignacia had to pay.

"I'm sorry," he said. He had the feeling this wasn't a good way to start with a girlfriend.

Wind over Heaven

The taxi pulled away, kicking up yellow dust. Ignacia showed him where the corrugated tin roof jutted out of the hillside. She guided him slowly down the trail. His feet barely grazed the ground. "Don't let go," he begged her.

"I've been waiting for you all my life," she said. "I won't let go."

He had never been curious about the details of love, and now he wished he'd paid more attention. Probably he should kiss her, but what would happen after that?

Below in the valley, the smog was so thick that Diego could barely see the outline of the Latin American Tower.

The outer walls of the shack were made of jerry cans pounded flat and nailed into place.

"I know it doesn't look like much. Don't worry."

"I was just remembering. Our room at the vecinidad was this small. And . . . I had these dreams. I had dreams when I was a little boy."

Inside, Ignacia lit a gas lamp. When she pulled aside the blankets that hung against the far side of the shack, Diego expected to see a wall of dirt. Instead a great blackness opened up. A cave.

He smelled the scent of water on stone, the exhalations of the earth.

"Come on," said Ignacia. She ducked behind the blankets, taking the light with her. He lingered for a moment, then followed, slowly, hardly able to scrape the ground with his shoes and move himself forward.

Sometimes they had to crawl or wriggle through narrow openings. But there were big rooms, too, extending beyond the reach of the lantern. There she would take him by the hand and pull him along. At one point they had to cross a narrow bridge of stone spanning a chasm. They crossed carefully, crawling, though Diego knew he wouldn't fall very fast if he did slip.

One of the rooms after that had a statue in it. It was of a woman holding an oil lamp. Diego stopped to look. Ignacia kept going with the lantern and he had to call her back.

"Who made it?" he asked.

"I did. That's my mother."

"It's very good."

"Come on, we're almost there."

In the next room, she set the lantern onto a ledge, pulled herself up, and helped Diego to follow her.

On the ledge sat a block of stone carved with the twinings of rattlesnakes. There were skulls in the design, too, that looked Aztec.

Ignacia pushed the top of the stone, and it slid away. The block

Bruce Holland Rogers

was in fact a lidded chest.

Very carefully, the fortune teller drew out a bundle. She unwrapped it and unfolded the brittle skin. Flakes fell from it.

On the skin were painted the figures of gods with white stars defining their bodies.

"A codex," Diego said. "I've seen them in books."

Ignacia moved the light so that the figures were easier to see. "The center reveals the names and motions of the stars. My mother's grandmother, who found these things, first learned to read the future from them."

She moved the light again. "These are the figures my mother didn't like. She wanted to keep this part of the codex from the world, when this is the part that the world needs most."

Diego could make little sense of the design. There was what looked like the head of a monster on a spit. The men in headdresses were Eagle Warriors and Jaguar Warriors, a little like the men in those dreams of his childhood. But what did these black footprints mean? Were these other figures priests? Severed limbs were scattered about them.

The central figure stood out among all these elaborately dressed figures. It was the spare outline of a naked man. In his hands, the man held a blue severed head. Stars spilled from its eyes.

All around were the bars and dots of numbers.

"Is this Mayan?" he asked.

"Aztec, mostly. Mexica."

"But the numbers . . ."

"Are Mayan, yes. It's strange that way, like no other codex."

"It's probably not a real one," Diego told her.

"No. It's no forgery. A marriage, maybe. A blending." She pointed to the outline of the naked man. "This Empty One is you. Here are the stars and day names of your birth, and your mother's birth. See how you were foretold?"

He wondered if now would be a good time to kiss her, but he felt himself lifting up from the cave floor.

"Stay put!" Ignacia scolded.

"I don't know how." It felt like he might get so light that he would dissolve into air.

She grabbed his shirt and hauled him down.

"Every fifty-two years," she said, nodding at the codex, "the priests had to renew the sun. The Fifth Sun. Human beings live in the fifth attempt at creation. Every fifty-two years, the sun is exhausted, and on the last night of the cycle the priests would labor to feed it, restore it."

Wind over Heaven

"Sacrifice." That was another thing he had seem when he was a child, blood on the temple steps. Blood and clouds of flies. He felt sick.

"Yes. But some day, even that would not be enough. No sun is eternal. So the priests who had seen deep into the smoke of creation devised a plan. They would find the Empty One and bring him to this cave. If the sun failed to rise, the Empty One would stir the Head of Heaven." She pointed at the blue head pictured in the codex. "The stars reside inside that vessel. As below, so above. When the Empty One stirred the vessel, his actions would rearrange the stars in the sky."

"Would that make me stop floating?" His voice sounded thin to him, as if air were trying to speak.

"That will reinvent everything. As below, so above. When the stars swing in new constellations, the world they rule will be different. There will be a different past, a different future. Every branch of creation will have taken a different turn. It will be a different Fifth Sun, perhaps a stronger one. Who knows? Everything will be different!" She let go of him to reach into the chest. "This is the vessel."

It was blue, shaped like the head of a God. Maybe Tlaloc. Diego had seen him in the museum.

Ignacia pulled him down again. "Take it."

The blue head began to glow as Diego's hands closed around it.

"If I shake it," he said, "that will make me heavy again?"

"That will transform the world," Ignacia said.

The head seemed to get lighter in his hands. It became translucent and slippery. His hands did, too. He could barely hold on to it.

"If you don't shake it, now that you have touched it, you will die," she said.

He felt tricked. Maybe she wouldn't make such a good girlfriend after all.

Her fingers slipped through the material of his shirt. He rose, drifted out of her reach. He really was turning into air.

Diego could see stars glowing inside the head. He recognized Orion, Scorpio, Auriga. Could Ignacia see them? She would call them by Nahuatl names.

"The sun has not failed," he said.

"The sun is exhausted. Look at the miserable world it shines upon! Everything has gone wrong!"

Diego's misty hands trembled. The misty stars inside the head rippled like lights on water.

Bruce Holland Rogers

Ignacia said, "You will *die!* Shake it!"

"You can't make me do it," he said. He looked at the jar, at the different colors of the stars. It would be pretty to see them dance around.

"Everything depends on it!" she shouted. She threw a handful of dust at him, and it went right through him. "You have to do it!"

"No I don't," he said.

And then he did it. He swirled the jar. The stars inside broke free and spun like bright seeds in a whirlwind.

"Yes!" cried Ignacia. "It is done."

Diego watched the stars settle into their new positions. As they did so, he floated back to the ledge. The head grew opaque, and Ignacia pulled it out of his hands. "You almost ruined everything," she said as she put the head away.

She stepped down from the ledge and took up the lantern. She didn't wait to see if he was coming, and he had to hurry to keep up with the light. He seemed to have his full weight back.

They emerged from the cave into bright sunshine. The shack was gone.

At the bottom of the valley, there was a city. But it wasn't Mexico City. There were thin lines of land over the water, and thin lines of water across the land. Causeways and canals. On the canals, Diego could see boats moving.

There was a mountain where no mountain should be. But it wasn't a mountain.

"The Great Temple," he said. "They've built it even bigger."

"No," said Ignacia. "You can't think of the world you knew. Aztecs didn't build that. Not under these stars. We don't know who these people are." She smiled. "Everything's new. And I did it. I made it happen."

Diego noticed the tree. He stepped over to it, reached up and picked one of the fruits. It looked like an enormous strawberry.

"Everything is different," Ignacia warned. "We don't know how anything works. We don't know the names of things. We don't know what we can eat and what is poison." As she said these words, he could see a change in her face.

"It's all right," he said, and bit into the fruit. Beneath thick skin, it was sweet and tender.

Wind stirred the air, and its motions carried a voice that said, "Tsikay daineuzlatl."

"Did you hear that?" said Ignacia.

"It's the wind," Diego said. "He tells us, 'I am your breath.'"

She stared at him.

"I don't think I want you to be my girlfriend," he said. He finished the fruit and picked another one. "Maybe I'll meet someone in Maceolacán." And when he saw she didn't understand, he pointed to it. "The city."

He stopped eating to look inside his wallet. Still full of feathers.

"Here," he said, putting a few of them on the ground for her. "I owe you for the taxi."

She looked at the feathers as if she didn't understand what they were for. She'd get it figured out after a while. He finished the fruit and wiped his hands on his pants. Then he started down the hill.

"Where are you going?" she said.

"To the market." A bright green bird flew over — a little treasure house with wings. It made him laugh.

"Why are you laughing?" she demanded.

He turned to face her. She clutched her feathers so angrily that she was going to damage them, and then they wouldn't buy as much. "I'm going to find someone who can read the stars," he said. "A fortune teller." He laughed again. "Four green heixtotl feathers for my lucky numbers. Six to answer a question about love."

These Shoes Strangers Have Died Of

Nineteen forty-two was the first summer of the war bond campaign. After the newsreels and before the feature, a government clip showed a Japanese soldier bayoneting a Chinese baby. The voice-over said again and again, "Buy a bond. Kill a Jap. Buy a bond. Kill a Jap."

The rifle with its bayonet rose and fell. People coming out of the theater later would look at me, a young man old enough to shave. Some of them asked me outright why I hadn't enlisted.

"I'll be old enough in September," I'd say.

After the theater was empty, I'd sweep the aisles and then sit in one of the middle seats, the popular ones even on slow nights and matinees. I'd close my eyes grip the wooden armrests. Beneath my palms the joy and fear and anger and relief that others had felt in this theater moved in the wood grain like a nest of animals, stirring.

Buy a bond. Kill a Jap.

Feelings like a knot you can't begin to untie.

"Kill a Jap. Be a Jap," I said to the curtained screen.

‡

The house I live in now was built to my own design on the north-facing slope of a canyon where the trees grow dense and dark. The first floor is half buried so that the second floor won't rise above the trees, won't too easily reveal the house. To drive here, you must follow a pair of wheel ruts that turn off from the gravel road five miles distant. Unless you know where to look, underbrush hides the way. I stay put in winter. For five months of the year, the snow between house and road lies undisturbed.

On the second floor is a corner room without windows. There's a deadbolt on the door to that room, and a padlock. Inside, a Nazi battle flag hangs on one wall alongside photos of the camps. Black and white photos of the living and the dead. The far side of that

Wind over Heaven

wall is devoted to wartime posters of buck-toothed Japanese. There's a photo of me as I was in 1943, a new-minted soldier, posing with fixed bayonet and glaring at the camera as if the lens were Tojo himself.

Buy a bond. Kill a Jap.

The war, my war is limited to that wall. The other walls are papered with photographs of skulls stacked in Cambodia, bodies swelling in the sun of Burundi or Rwanda, mass graves opened like ripe fruit split wide to spill their seeds. Some of the newspaper images have yellowed. Some are fresh.

Nina, my agent, has seen the locked door, but has never asked what's on the other side. She has other things on her mind. "Build a studio in Boulder or Denver," she says to me twice a year. "You'd be close to the galleries. All of this would be so much *easier*."

She wants me out of the mountains. If I had a heart attack, a stroke, no one would know unless I radioed for help myself. Park County Rescue would have to travel the same pair of wheel ruts that Nina's hired truck negotiates, spring and fall, when it comes to take my work to the galleries.

"I can hunt deer from my front porch," I tell her. "Could I do that in Denver or Boulder?"

In the closet of the locked room, I keep the shoes, the boots, the uniforms.

The shoes are flattened, sun-cracked — a right shoe hidden among high weeds in El Salvador, a left shoe I stole from Bergen-Belsen, a right that I dug from the rotting mud of Cambodia. Shoes strangers have died of. Shoes that fit me. I only keep the ones that do.

Some of the boots are like the shoes — dry-rotted, split-seamed. The others go with the uniforms, patent leather boots hand-polished until they gleam like black glass.

A full-length mirror hangs on the inside of the closet door.

Several of the uniforms are simple: fatigues of the Ugandan security forces, the Khmer Rouge, Brazilian or Chilean troops assigned to domestic duty. Khaki is interchangeable with tan, with gray, with blue.

It's the black uniform that I prize above the others. It's the black that I dress in to stand before the mirror. On the World War II wall, young men in dress uniforms like this one smile easy smiles.

I smile their smiles for the mirror, feeling what is natural to feel in such a uniform. Invincibility. Pride. The twin lightning bolts on the collar have everything and nothing to do with history. The death's head in the band of the cap is timeless.

Bruce Holland Rogers

To my smiling reflection, I say, "What are we to do with you? What is to be done?" The question is no abstraction. It's a practical matter. It's the question I must ask each day before I begin to carve.

Today, though, it's more practical than ever.

Downstairs on my couch is a young man, bound and gagged.

What am I to do with him?

The silver skull insignia gleams.

I hang the uniform and dress for work.

‡

Snow covers the studio skylight. The shadows are soft, deep, and blue. Before turning on the lights, I run my hands over the rough-hewn block.

When I begin a new piece, even when I can feel into the wood and know exactly what I'm cutting down to, the first hours of work are always a struggle. The wood resists. Chisels skip off, and saw blades twist out of shape as if I were trying to cut my way through granite. I have to prove myself each time, coax the echoes from the grain.

Then, once I have the shape roughed out, the heartwood softens, yields, invites me in. My blades melt through crosscuts as if I were carving butter. The wood guides the tools, and the face, the shoulder, the hand emerges.

For the piece I am working on today, the early stage lasts a long time. The wood is green. Ordinarily, I cure the wood before I work, but in this case, I don't have the time. Resin sticks to my tools.

After two hours of work in the studio, I brush the sawdust from my coveralls and come downstairs to have a look at him. His eyes are wide, but it's hard to say if what I see in them is fear. He's young. Young, but old enough to shave.

Hanging near the stove where I put them out to dry are his black jeans, black t-shirt, and motorcycle boots. He wears the jeans and work shirt I dressed him in, a size too large.

His hands, tied together, rest in his lap. The knuckles of his left hand are tattooed with F-U-C-K, and the right with K-I-L-L. Though his feet are tied together, he has kicked the books from one of my shelves, the only damage he's been at liberty to do. Shirer, Arendt, Camus. History and philosophy in a little pile at his feet.

I say, "If only you had a match, right?"

He glares. I watch him breathe.

It seems to me as if the wooden faces in the room are watching him too — the teak faces locked in screams, the anguished expressions in pine or spruce or ebony. All the hollow wooden eyes take him in.

Untying the gag is like breaking a dam. Obscenities flow from him like water.

"I wouldn't have to gag you," I tell him, "if you could keep a civil tongue."

"Fuck you."

I remind him that I saved his life.

"Fuck if you did," he says. "They'd have come back for me."

"I told you. There have been no new tracks in the snow. They haven't been back."

"Fuck you," he says, but he must know his confederates, must understand the truth as I tell it to him.

"You'd be frozen solid without me," I say, "so whatever I do to you now, it's better than that, right? It's better than being dead."

I force the gag back into his mouth before he can answer. If I don't, he'll shout his lungs out and I won't be able to concentrate.

I go back to work.

‡

I earn more for Nina than all of her other clients combined. If she worries that I will have a heart attack, it is only because of the money.

She is not without compassion, but some of the things she has done for me have hardened her. The Auschwitz crossbeam was one.

I grant few interviews. Shouldn't the work speak for itself? But sometimes an interview brings its surprises. I once regretted aloud that there was no wood from Auschwitz for me to carve. A month after my words were in print, Nina had a call from the Israeli government. They'd have preferred a Jewish artist, but no one else achieves my effects.

The crossbeam came from one of the barracks torn down after the war. It had, for a time, supported the roof of a Polish barn.

When they flew me in to inspect it, I did not ask how the beam had come to Israel, to a warehouse where it lay in a military truck bed like a missile.

The Deputy Minister of Culture, standing before the truck, waved some documentation under my nose. I stepped past him and touched the wood. Even after forty years, it was alive with ghosts.

"We will give it to you," he said, "on the condition that you cut it in half and produce two finished works, one of which you will return to us. For the memorial."

I agreed.

They could not know how dense the wood was with tortured faces, with gestures of pain and despair. Back in the States, I cut the beam in half, as agreed. Then I split each half lengthwise and carved four pieces instead of two. Let the Israelis imagine that I'd had to carve deep to find the images I gave them. Let them think the missing wood littered the floor of my studio as chips and dust.

All four finished pieces were a tangled knot of victims.

Nina told me, "You can't sell the extras. You'll give yourself away."

"We will sell them," I said. "Sealed bids. Secret bids. We'll give slides for Hauptmann to circulate among likely buyers."

Nina's arms were crossed. "Not Hauptmann. I won't go through Hauptmann again. Even talking to him on the phone, I feel dirty."

"So write him. Mail him the slides."

"But the bidders he will bring us. . . ."

"It's what I want, Nina."

"This is the last time I go through Hauptmann."

I said nothing. No one else knew the people Hauptmann knew.

A month later, Nina flung the list at my face. "Do you see where these bids are coming from? Do you *see*?"

I picked up the loose pages from my floor, looked at the names and offers. "Here," I said, and pointed at a bid from El Salvador. "This can only be Rosado himself. It's not the highest bid, but I want you to sell it to him."

"If we weren't using Hauptmann's list, I could find someone else," Nina said. "A collector. An investor who would put it away in a vault for his heirs. The money would be better, and—"

"Sell it to Rosado."

"In God's name, why?" Nina said. "Why do you want someone like him to have it?"

"If I'm lucky," I said, "he'll install it over his bed."

Nina's face was pale.

"Sell it to him, Nina. In a way, it's his already."

Then I picked another bid, one Nina liked no better.

The last carving we sold openly to the Museum of Modern Art.

‡

Once or twice a year, I look for trees in the killing fields. Some are old fields. Some are fresh. I walk around the tree trunks, touching them, feeling for the echoes. Then I direct the cutting of the logs that will be shipped to the States, trucked from Denver to the house and studio in the mountains.

Usually, the freshest sources are the hardest to get to. Not always, though. Not always.

Wind over Heaven

‡

A logging road runs parallel to my canyon, on the other side of the ridge. If I have unwelcome visitors, that's usually where they come from.

The night I found my guest, I was reading. I heard the crack of a rifle shot.

I turned my lights off, shut down the generator.

Snow was falling. It had been coming down for hours in a fine powder, the sort of snow that continues, steadily, all through one day and into the next.

When I stepped outside, I could hear their voices at the top of the ridge.

There was another shot. Youthful laughter. Raised voices.

Then silence.

When at last I heard one of the voices again, there was no mirth in it. Indistinct words. Then another voice, pleading.

Again, silence. Enduring silence.

I waited a long time before getting the kerosene lantern out and putting on my boots. Ordinary boots. Sorels. I had no way of knowing that something special would be waiting for me at the top of the ridge.

Lighting my way with the lantern, I found my way up the slope to a small clearing. Fresh snowfall hadn't yet covered the shell casings and beer bottles that appeared in the lantern's circle of yellow light.

A shadow caught my eye, and I extended the lantern toward it. Stretched out on bloody snow was a body. The bald head was uncovered. Vapor clouds of breath rose from the face. The eyes were closed.

An old man, I thought. Lantern light is tricky. It took a moment for me to see that, no, his face was unlined. He was young. Stepping closer, I saw the swastikas tattooed on his arm.

When I leaned to see his face, my hand fell upon the trunk, and I paused, taking it all in.

‡

I got my first taste of fighting in the fall of '44, in the Hürtgen Forest. The trees of the Hürtgen were still just trees to me then. I had the same feelings for them any infantryman would. When they gave cover to my unit's advance, I loved them. When German shells exploded among the branches over our heads, they rained down limbs heavy as stones, splinters sharp as shrapnel. We grenade-felled trees to clear booby traps, to build an instant bridge over tangles of barbed wire. Trees were obstacles, trees were useful. The tang of fresh resin filled the air.

I paid more attention to the Germans.

Up close, as I stepped over them, the German dead in the Hürtgen could have been my cousins. Even after news of Malmédy, I didn't hate them. I understood what had to be done. I did it.

Buy a bond. Kill a Jap.

Kill a Jerry. A Nazi.

‡

The swastika tattoos on the kid's arms are sharp-edged and very black. He hasn't had them long.

"Do you know what I think?" I say to him. I haven't removed the gag this time. His eyes bore into me.

"I think," I tell him, "that when a victim isn't handy, one needs to be manufactured. Am I right?"

His eyes narrow. His gaze shifts to the deer rifle by the door, but even if he unties himself while I'm upstairs, he'll find that it's unloaded.

"I'm lucky that you and your companions didn't know I was here — an old man living alone. An artist with shelves of history books. I'd have been a more interesting victim, don't you think? I'd have been perfect. You might be drinking a beer with them right now, remembering, laughing. Instead, you had a little surprise. Like Röhm's surprise. You know about Röhm, of course, about what happened to him. You know all about the turn things can take."

His lips work around the gag, but he's only trying to swallow. There's no question, no understanding in his eyes.

"Ah. Never heard of Ernst Röhm. Well. It's an old, old story. Your friends, your compatriots, they really did surprise you, yes?"

He doesn't nod, but emotions play over his face like shadows. He was surprised. He still doesn't understand it.

"Your strength is that you might do anything." I lower my voice, lean toward him. "Anything." I smile. "But that's the danger, too. Do you understand? Hitler purged his lieutenants. You should know that. You should know what history can teach you about yourself."

From the books on the floor, I select Shirer's *Rise and Fall*. "We could start here," I say hefting the thick volume. "Shall I read you a chapter? Shall we begin at the beginning?"

Oh, the hate in his eyes.

"No," I say. "That's not the right sort of history for you. You need something tailored to you, yes? Something more personal, more relevant to your present situation. In fact, let's not call it history at all. Let's call it a crime story, set in the winter of '44. A crime story. A puzzle. I'll give you the crime. You tell me the motive."

‡

The snow was deep, and in places the wind was piling it deeper still. Here and there, it came up to my belt.

I held my rifle at port arms and kept a good ten feet between myself and my prisoner. I doubted that he'd try to jump me for the gun — his own lines were far away, now, melting back into Germany — but SS soldiers were a cocky lot.

I wished for tire ruts to walk in. Even with the prisoner blazing the trail, wading through the snow was wearing me out, and we were still a long hike from Battalion HQ.

I heard, like an answered prayer, the sound of engines. A couple of jeeps emerged from the forest below and turned toward us. The paths left by their churning wheels invited me, and I thought, *Hallelujah!*

Planning to wait for the jeeps to pass, I said to the prisoner, "Hold up. Halt."

An explosion belted my gut like a sucker punch. I hit the deck, but the German remained standing, hands still clasped calmly behind his head. He smirked at me.

"*Nur eine Landmine,*" he said in a voice that might be explaining thunder to a child. "*Nichts befürchten.*"

Memory is tricky. That probably isn't exactly what he said. I did not learn German until after the war.

One of the jeeps was upside down, and the snow had been blown clear for ten feet around it.

I stood up and let my rifle point more emphatically at the German while I brushed snow from the front of my jacket with my other hand.

Around us trees swayed in the wind.

"Okay," I said as deeply as I could manage. "Now march!"

A third jeep had pulled up behind the other two, then turned around to go back for medics. Running down the opposite slope of the valley, churning snow before him like a plow, was some GI who must have popped out of a foxhole. He was shouldering an aidman's bag.

I didn't have to hurry my prisoner. He waded forward resolutely, as if eager to draw closer.

One of the jeep's passengers, an infantryman, was lying face down in the crater. He had no legs. Another guy was lying beside the tree trunk he'd been thrown against, and nothing but his mouth was moving. He said, "Jesus, sweet Jesus," again and again.

Bruce Holland Rogers

The third man, a lieutenant, lay on his back with the jeep pinning his chest. The aidman leaned close to see if he was breathing.

He wasn't.

Clicking his tongue as we passed, my prisoner said, and this I'm almost sure of, "*Daß ist also das Kriegsglück.*"

The aidman looked up. There was an 82nd Airborne patch on his shoulder. "What did he say?"

"I don't know," I admitted. "I don't speak German."

From the other jeep, a man said, "Thinks he's clever, don't he?"

It was true. The German was smirking as he surveyed the scene.

The dead lieutenant looked asleep, eyes half closed, mouth slack. He was young, a ninety-day wonder.

"You take that Jerry son of a bitch into the woods," the aidman told me, "and you shoot that grin off his goddamn face."

The prisoner shook his head very slightly and clicked his tongue again. I prodded him with the gun barrel. "Stop that shit. Keep moving."

The aidman crouched beside the man who'd been thrown against the tree, but over his shoulder he said, "If you were Airborne, you'd take my advice."

It was easier to walk in the tire ruts.

A while later, the jeep that had gone back for help came rolling through the snow, ferrying medics to where the mine had blown the first jeep. They drove slowly, staying in the tracks, wary of another mine. We stood aside to let them through.

Very quietly, the prisoner started singing, bobbing his head in time with the song. It was a march. It was a true believer's song.

"Knock it off," I said to his back.

He stopped, but before long he had started it up again.

"Come on," I said. "You've made your point."

He stopped singing, but he still bobbed his head from side to side, and he turned slightly, awkwardly because his hands were still clasped behind his neck. I saw enough of his face to see the smirk again.

"What is it with you?" I said. "Halt!"

He stopped and turned full around to face me.

We stood, watching each other.

His eyes were the color of ice, of winter skies.

"Let's take a detour. Up there." I gestured with my head, up the slope, away from the tire ruts.

He unclasped his hands and pointed, tentatively, over his head.

"You got it," I said. "Let's go."

Wind over Heaven

As we walked, wading again through deep drifts, he began once again to sing. Loudly. This time, I didn't shut him up.

The further we went, the more densely the pine trees crowded around us.

Remember, this is a mystery. Why was I doing this? I can tell you, it wasn't the Malmédy massacre. And all the rest, all the rumors, smacked of propaganda.

I made him stop, then turn to face me.

The trees circled us like witnesses.

I brought the M1 to my shoulder and pointed it at his chest.

"Doctor's orders," I told him, "courtesy of the 82nd Airborne."

I watched where I was aiming — the center of his chest.

The rifle report echoed from the surrounding hills.

He pitched back and hardly kicked. It had been a clean shot, a hunter's shot. His back arched for a moment, then fell.

Then, when it was too late, I wanted to know what his face had been like before I had shot him. Was he surprised? Was he smirking?

I couldn't tell. Dead, his face was a mask.

My knees got weak. I knelt next to him in the snow.

There was a secret here.

The smell of blood was like copper in the cold air. I thought of hunting again, of killing and dressing out deer, spilling their steaming guts onto the snow.

I detached my bayonet, opened his coat and shirt, unbuckled his belt. A bayonet is not a hunting knife. It's made for stabbing, not slicing. The blade is too long for good leverage. But I made it do, opening him up, spilling him out, looking for clues. Blood up to my elbows.

Months later, when we began to liberate the camps, I told myself that there was justice in what I had done. But the killing preceded the motive. Even though I had heard the rumors, I only believed in the camps when I saw them myself.

‡

"So," I say to him, "it's a mystery, isn't it? Why did I kill him?"

He had listened intently. I pat his leg, and he doesn't try to kick me.

"And here you are, another mystery. Another Nazi, delivered into my hands. But things are different. I didn't kill you, I saved you. What for? What happens next?"

His eyes are wide.

‡

There is more. After I dressed out the SS trooper and strung his

Bruce Holland Rogers

unreadable entrails across the snow, I pulled off his boots.

My hands were sticky. I washed them with snow, then undid my laces with numb fingers.

I had to stamp down hard to get his boots to fit my feet.

I walked around him, in his own boots, searching. Then I happened to rest my hand on the trunk of a pine tree.

And I felt him inside.

If the bayonet was a bad hunting knife, it was even worse for carving. At best, I could only strip the bark in the place where my trembling fingers detected him. But he was there. If I could free him of the wood, I would know what his face had looked like in his last moment.

But I lacked the tools.

For the rest of the war, I kept finding other faces in other trees. At Stavelot, where the SS had shot Belgian children, I found a face in a garden birch tree. In broken French, I explained. A farmer lent me his hand ax, and I did the detail work with another man's pocket knife.

The farmer, watching me work, watching the face that emerged, shed quiet tears. The face, I was made to understand, was his niece's.

Many times since the war, I have searched the Ardennes forest. I have never been able to find the spot where I killed the trooper. I have never been able to find the tree.

‡

I remove his gag.

He says nothing.

I say, "That's better. That's much better."

He is looking at the wooden faces, shaking his head. "It's bullshit," he says at last. "I don't fucking believe you."

"What part don't you believe?"

"Ghosts," he says. "I don't believe in ghosts."

"Not ghosts," I tell him. "That's not what they are."

I go back to the studio to work, to finish what I have worked on all the time that he's been here.

‡

Really, it is necessary to wear the uniform, to pull those shining boots over your calves and pose and smile. I have the Luger that matches the uniform. It is not a heavy gun, but without the weight of it in its glossy holster, the uniform and its truth are incomplete.

The commander of SS troops at Malmédy, at Stavelot, was Lt. Col. Jochen Peiper. Sentenced to hang, confident of reprieve, he called the war "a proud and heroic time. Wherever we stood was

Wind over Heaven

Germany, and as far as my tank gun reached was my kingdom."
   The boots are proud and heroic.
   The holster is proud and heroic.
   The insignia gleam.

‡

When I come downstairs again, he has freed his hands and is working at the ropes that bind his feet. He hears me coming, but seems unconcerned until he looks up and sees the uniform.
   I unholster the Luger.
   He hardly seems to notice the boots and canvas bag I carry in my other hand. All his attention is on the gun.
   "Isn't it beautiful?" I say, but I mean the uniform, not the gun. "Go on." I wave the muzzle at him casually. "It's time for us to go. Finish untying yourself."
   He doesn't move.
   "Come on," I tell him. "I haven't got all day."
   "What are you going to do?"
   "Shut up," I tell him, "and get those ropes off your feet."
   When he has freed himself, I tell him to stand. He grunts and holds his side where he must have taken a kick to the ribs. I make him strip and dress in his own clothes. All but his boots.
   "Wear these," I say. I toss the boots — very much like the ones I am wearing, only these ones do not shine. They are boots that have seen the battlefield. They are scarred. The leather is cracked.
   I say, "You can't get them on by staring at them."
   He had no coat when I found him. I tell him to bring the blanket from the couch. It's an old woolen one that I won't miss.
   "Now out," I say. "Back to where I found you."
   "I'm thirsty," he says, "and hungry."
   "If you had the gun and I were the one who was hungry, would you feed me?"
   He thinks about it. "Yes."
   "All right." I herd him into the kitchen. Without taking my eyes from him, I get down a box of crackers. At the sink, he drinks water from his cupped hands. Then he eats a handful of the crackers.
   "That's enough," I say. "Take the box. Eat them later."
   The snow has gone on falling almost all the time he's been with me. I can find no tracks. The snow is up to our knees.
   We need a tune for marching. I whistle the regimental march of the *Leibstandarte Adolf Hitler*.
   Very quietly, he says, "Please."
   I stop whistling.
   We march.

Bruce Holland Rogers

He says, "What will happen?"

I say, "What are we to do with the killers, with the people who are filled with hate?"

"I never killed anyone," he says.

"But you have hurt people. Don't ask me to believe that you haven't done that."

I start to whistle the march again. Then I stop to say, "Do you know that in Germany, that music is illegal? They'll throw you in jail just for carrying the tune. There's a long list of forbidden music. What do you think of that?"

He says, "I don't understand you. Who *are* you?"

By which he must mean, *Whose side are you on?*

‡

Once I was at a gallery opening of my recent work. This set of sculptures had been especially demanding. Like the Auschwitz crossbeams, each piece incorporated a score of twisted faces, a hundred twisted limbs. Drawing them out had exhausted me. I could hardly stand to look at them.

The wood had come from Cambodian trees.

The gallery was full. Patrons had wine glasses in their hands as they went from one piece to another. Sometimes an art opening is noisy as a cocktail party. Mine tend to be subdued. This one was silent.

Nina and the gallery owner had already seen the pieces, and I was relieved to find, as I stood in the middle of the room with them, that they, like me, were in the mood for something else, anything else. We managed to hold a conversation in the middle of the room, focusing on each other, ignoring the little wooden hells that were all around us. And it worked. Before long we really did forget ourselves.

The gallery owner said something that struck me as funny. I laughed. I put my head back and roared.

A woman wheeled from one of the sculptures and shouted, "How can you laugh in here? How *can* you?"

‡

It is easy for me to find the spot on the ridge where I had found him. There's the stump of the pine tree that I felled while he was still unconscious.

"Stand there," I say. "Right where I found you."

He doesn't move.

I wave the pistol and say, "Come on."

He looks at me, hesitates, then steps sideways to the spot.

"I don't know about you," I say. "I don't know how far gone you might be, how you got started down this path."

"You won't—"

"Shut up," I say. "It doesn't matter whether I know or not. I only have one answer. There's only one thing for me to do about you and others like you."

I toss him the canvas bag. Catching it, he drops the box of crackers.

"Open it up," I say, and he does. He takes out the sculpture of the hand, and he doesn't know what to make of it until he turns it the right way, can see the meaning of the outstretched fingers, the unmistakable gesture.

Please. I'm hurt. I'm down. No more. Please.

"I took it out of the tree," I tell him, nodding at the stump.

With his free hand, he touches his side where his ribs still ache. His expression seems more angry than sad, more vengeful than softened with wisdom. But who knows?

He opens his mouth, begins to form a word.

"No," I say. "It doesn't matter. We're finished already."

He looks at the boots on his feet. The boots strangers have died of. When he looks up, I'm pointing the pistol at his chest. I watch his face. His expression is impossible to read.

I turn away, begin to retrace my steps. I, too, wear boots. The lustrous leather clings to my calves like a second skin, and melting snow beads up on the blackness to glint like the stars coming out. One point of light. Then another. Then one more. Soon, they will be numberless as the dead. And as cold.

Printed in the United States
4569